BUCKET LIST

MAPLE SYRUP MYSTERIES

EMILY JAMES

STRONGHOLD BOOKS

This is a work of fiction. I made it up. You are not in my book. I probably don't even know you. If you're confused about the difference between real life and fiction, you might want to call a counselor rather than a lawyer because names, characters, places, and incidents in this book are a product of my twisted imagination. Real locales and public names are sometimes used for atmospheric purposes. Any resemblance to actual people, living or dead, or to businesses, companies, events, and institutions is completely coincidental.

Editor: Christopher Saylor at www.saylorediting.wordpress.com/services/

Cover Design: Deranged Doctor Design at www.derangeddoctordesign.com

Published December 2017 by Stronghold Books

Ebook ISBN: 978-1-988480-16-9

Print ISBN: 978-1-988480-17-6

ALSO BY EMILY JAMES

Maple Syrup Mysteries

Sapped: A Maple Syrup Mysteries Prequel

A Sticky Inheritance

Bushwhacked

Almost Sleighed

Murder on Tap

Deadly Arms

Capital Obsession

Tapped Out

Bucket List

End of the Line

Rooted in Murder (Coming Soon!)

Cupcake Truck Mysteries

Sugar and Vice

Other Mysteries

Slay Bells Ringing

(contains a Maple Syrup Mysteries novella and a Cupcake Truck Mysteries novella)

For my dear friend Katie. It takes a lot of courage to do things your own way.

Worse than telling a lie is spending the rest of your life staying true to a lie.

— ROBERT BRAULT

1

I wouldn't have thought I was the type of person to be excited about a wooden door, but I almost felt like dancing in the frost-touched leaves when the door to the new, historically accurate sugar shack stayed open on its own.

Considering that I'd almost died, trapped inside the original sugar shack when it burned down, making sure that the door on the new one didn't slide shut randomly had been a priority for me.

Russ slid it shut, then opened it again one more time.

Watching it made me feel like I could take a full breath for the first time after having the wind knocked out of me. I could finally set free the fear that came with the memories of that day.

"I made sure the contractor leveled the ground," Russ said. "Even if the mechanism on the door gives out, gravity won't be pulling it closed anymore."

He waddled through the doorway, his barrel-shaped body rocking side to side more now than ever. His breathing wheezed. I doubted Russ had ever been a thin man, but he'd put on forty pounds since I'd met him a year ago.

He dropped into the nearest chair, and it groaned under him even though it was one of the few new items in the place. I'd spent the last two months sourcing period pieces to replace ones we'd lost in the fire. We'd finally be able to put the sugar shack back into our tours—which meant we'd be getting bookings from school groups again soon.

Russ leaned over his knees, but his wheezy breathing didn't ease. The excitement drained out of me and left a trail of tension behind it.

I knelt down beside him. "Are you okay?"

He shook his head. "Just tired from the walk here."

The walk here had taken us less than five minutes. As much as I didn't want to spoil the joy of finally reopening the historical sugar shack, maybe it was time I talked to Russ about his health.

The problem was I had no idea how to open a conversation like that. It seemed nosy to even think about it, given how very private Russ tended to be. "Do you think maybe you should see a doctor?"

Russ grunted. "I've already seen one. He didn't tell me anything I didn't already know. Lose weight. Take my medications regularly."

Medications plural. The last I'd heard, Russ only took high blood pressure medication. "He put you on something new?"

"A few of the numbers on my blood test were high. But I'm nearly seventy. What does he expect?" He pointed across the room. "I had Dave set the tools up a little different from how they were before. He's looking forward to running his first tour. He says meeting more people will help him create characters, whatever that means."

Trying to distract me with Dave's growing role at Sugarwood and his eccentricities as a writer weren't going to work. "What new medications did he prescribe you?"

He got back to his feet with a groan. "You don't need to worry about me."

Clearly I did because it seemed he wasn't worrying enough about himself. Maybe if he'd been only my business partner I could have agreed with him, but he wasn't. He'd become like family. My Uncle Stan had been my only uncle, and I didn't have any aunts. Russ had stepped into that role for me. The thought of losing him, too, made my chest hurt.

I followed him out of the sugar shack. "Just promise me you're taking your meds at least."

His gaze shifted to the side like he was trying to spot something he could distract me with.

My phone rang. If I didn't know it wasn't sentient, I would have suspected it of conspiring against me with Russ.

I swiped my finger across the screen. "This is Nikki."

This conversation isn't over, I mouthed to Russ.

The person on the other end of the line didn't respond immediately. I knew they were still there, though. I could hear them breathing and sniffling. For a second, I thought it might be a prank call and I considered hanging up.

"Is this Nicole Fitzhenry-Dawes?" a vaguely familiar man's voice said. "The one who was looking for a vintage 1800s maple syrup bucket?"

The timing was ideal. That bucket was the last piece we'd been missing. Not surprisingly, wooden items didn't age as well as metal ones. I'd found many of the metal tools within the first few weeks. The large pots used to evaporate the sap had taken me longer. Buckets and wooden sap spires had been elusive.

I'd finally turned to the curator-owner of the local chainsaw and logging museum for help. It seemed I'd been right to think he'd have sources that I didn't.

"That's me. Were you able to find one?"

"Yes, but...you're also a lawyer, right? You said you used to defend people back in DC."

That didn't sound pertinent to my bucket, but I had told him that when he asked what brought me to the area. "That's right."

A sharp exhale. "I need to hire you. I think I need to hire you. The police are out at my place. I was hoping you could come."

I wanted to exclaim *what?!* But I held it in.

Granted, you couldn't tell if someone was a potential law-breaker by looking at them, but the curator of the logging museum —Clement Dodd—wouldn't have even made my top ten list of people I'd suspect of committing a crime.

He was a big man and bearded like a lumberjack, but I had a suspicion he grew the beard because he ran a chainsaw and logging museum and he knew that sort of thing would make his establishment more memorable. It was the part he played. He'd also worn round glasses that looked too small for his face, and when I'd come into the museum, he'd been reading a book on the War of 1812.

The museum was his "early retirement," he'd told me. Prior to moving back to Fair Haven, he'd curated larger museums and then taught college history classes for a few years. Even though I'd only come to ask for help locating a sap bucket, he'd taken me around the museum. He'd been prone to staring off into space like he forgot what he was saying, but his knowledge of each item had shamed me because I didn't know half as much about my business when I'd been running tours last winter.

Hopefully, whatever had brought the police out to his museum turned out to be a misunderstanding. Given his line of work, the most likely cause was that some piece in his museum turned out to be stolen property. That could be a tricky situation, but if his records were as meticulous as I suspected they were, it should be easy enough to demonstrate that he'd purchased the item instead of stealing it and to argue that he didn't know it was stolen.

"Since you're not sure if you need to hire me," I said, "how about you tell me what's going on first?"

"May I tell you while you're on your way?"

His voice was almost softer than mine. Soft voices were always harder to read than the average voice. They tended to hide fear a little better, in my experience. But I thought I might have caught a slight tremor.

It wouldn't cost me anything more than a little gas to head in his direction. I could do that for him. He'd been so helpful in narrowing down exactly what type of sap bucket I was looking for and helping track one down.

"Sure."

The chainsaw and logging museum was on the opposite side of Fair Haven from Sugarwood, but I could swing around the outskirts of town, avoiding most of the stop signs and traffic lights.

I hurried back down the path toward my house where my car was parked. "It shouldn't take me more than ten to fifteen minutes. You don't have to answer any questions the police have until I get there as long as you tell them your lawyer is coming, but if you weren't involved in whatever they're investigating, then it's a good idea to give them the information they ask for."

There was enough of a hesitation that my palms started to sweat. Maybe I'd read him wrong, and he was involved in something criminal. But I was sure I'd told him in our conversation before that I didn't want to defend people who were guilty anymore.

"What if I'm not sure?" he asked.

His voice had gone even softer, and I strained to hear him above the rustling of the last dry leaves still clinging to the trees overhead.

This wasn't a time for misunderstandings. "You're not sure you have anything useful to tell them?"

"I'm not sure whether I killed my employee or not."

2

The words *oh, crap* didn't seem nearly strong enough.

I picked up my pace to a near jog. It'd been one thing when I thought he might have accidentally purchased stolen goods. It was another thing entirely when the police were looking at him as a person of interest in a murder.

And how could he not know if he'd done it?

It was more likely that he did know and simply didn't want me to refuse to help him because he'd done it. Either way, I'd help him out now and then pass him along to Anderson Taylor, another defense attorney in the area who I'd formed a friendship with a few months back. I didn't defend guilty clients. Even if I was willing to, I wasn't a good choice. *Stage fright* would have been too mild a way of describing what happened to me when I got in front of a jury.

I slid into my car, and my phone synched to Bluetooth. "Did you tell the police that you aren't sure?"

"No one's asked me yet. I called you as soon as the police got here. They're taking my wife's statement now."

So he wasn't worried about his wife's involvement or about them asking her questions.

I turned out of Sugarwood's driveway and headed in the direction of the museum. The route only had two turns, so I didn't even need my GPS. "Calling a lawyer before they've even spoken to you is going to make you seem guilty even if you're not."

"I couldn't take the chance. My wife...she found me with his blood on my clothes, standing next to his body."

Not good. That not only screamed *guilty* but *liar* as well if he claimed he didn't know whether he'd killed his employee or not. I couldn't turn this case over to Anderson soon enough. If I wasn't on the phone with Clement, I might have called him right away.

As it was, my best option was to do damage control and make this easier for Anderson once he took over the case. "I need you to tell me—honestly—what happened. I need to be prepared when we talk to the police."

"That's what I've been telling you. I don't know what happened."

Unlike my last client, there wasn't any hostility or snarkiness in Clement's voice. It sounded more like hopelessness, like someone who'd given up.

I had a feeling I wasn't going to be able to sort through this in one short phone call. And it was sounding more and more like the best plan was to stonewall the police and not answer any of their questions at all. "When the police come to talk to you, tell them you don't want to answer any questions until your lawyer is present and that I'm already on my way."

We disconnected, and I instructed my phone to call Anderson. The call went to voicemail. I left a brief message.

I decided to bypass the turn I usually took onto a gravel road. It was the shorter path and more direct, but the speed limit on the paved road was faster. I should get there just as quickly as I normally did, but I wasn't quite as comfortable driving my new car yet as I had been with my old one. The steering and brakes were both more sensitive. I'd never live it down if I landed my new car in the ditch less than a month after buying it. Tony, my mechanic, would make some joke about adding training wheels if I did.

By the time I got to the museum parking lot, it was full of official vehicles and Mark's truck. In the last case I'd worked, I'd had the advantage of calling on Mark's medical wisdom to look at the autopsy results. We'd technically be on opposite sides this time.

At least for the short time I'd be working the case.

I tamped down on the flutters in my stomach that felt a bit like fireflies in a jar. My stomach clearly didn't realize that I wasn't staying on this case. Because I wasn't. Not even the lure of finally investigating something new after months of working entirely on Sugarwood business could make me take on a guilty client.

Clement sat outside the front of the museum on a chair carved out of a tree stump.

Troy Summoner, the youngest officer on the Fair Haven police force, stood next to him, like a gargoyle guarding a castle, his arms crossed and his face stern.

Then again, Troy's face always looked a little on the stern side. He was like Keanu Reeves in that his expression rarely changed. His happy face was nearly indistinguishable from his unhappy face.

Great for a police officer, but it probably wreaked havoc in his personal life. I could barely stand it when Mark wore sunglasses and I wasn't able to see and interpret the expression in his eyes.

I could tell when Troy spotted me because he lowered his arms and nodded at me. "I didn't know you were going to be his lawyer, Ms. Dawes."

I let the *Dawes* part slide. Most people in Fair Haven found Fitzhenry-Dawes too much of a mouthful. It would be so much easier when Mark and I married and I could change my last name to a simple Cavanaugh. I understood why my parents gave me the last name they did, but they hadn't considered how hard it would be for people to say—or the added challenge it would create for me in filling out forms, for that matter.

"I am," I said to Troy. "Who's in charge today?"

"Chief McTavish. I almost wish Sergeant Higgins and Officer Scott would stay away longer. I've been called into almost everything the past few days. I haven't gotten this much experience since former Chief Wilson."

Erik Higgins and Elise had surprised us all last month by declaring that they'd decided to get married in a small ceremony with only family and close friends. They'd taken a weekend away immediately after, and then a couple of days ago had headed off on a longer trip as a family. The situation with Elise's ex-husband had made them take a close look at their relationship and their future.

The way I'd heard the story, Elise tried to break up with Erik, saying she didn't want her children to get more attached to someone else they might lose if they broke up later on. Losing one father figure was bad enough. Erik responded by saying if they got married then the kids wouldn't need to worry about him leaving. Erik loved Arielle and Cameron almost as much as he loved Elise. They hadn't had a traditional proposal so much as a conversation, but when I thought about it, it suited both their personalities better than an elaborate proposal would have.

I peeked around Troy. Police personnel were still going in and out of the house like ants bringing back food for winter. "Did you want to tell the chief I'm here?"

Troy touched the button on his radio that activated the lapel mic clipped to his uniform. The Fair Haven police had been using the older hand-held style radios when I first came to Fair Haven, but one of the updates Chief McTavish had advocated for was the earpiece speakers and lapel mics to leave the officer's hands free.

Troy softly told whoever was on the other end that Mr. Dodd's lawyer was here and then moved a bit farther away.

I strode past him to where Clement hunched on the stump chair, staring off into the distance with a look that said he wasn't actually seeing anything. Up close, I understood why he was a suspect. Red splotches that looked like blood spatter covered his front all the way up to his face. He even had red flecks on his glasses. It wasn't the kind of pattern you saw on someone who'd been trying to help a victim. It was the kind you saw on the person who attacked the victim.

Oh please let him not have cut up his employee with one of the chainsaws or axes. Large parts of the museum looked like a serial killer's dream shopping store—historical chainsaws from as far back as the 1920s, axes of all shapes and sizes, single- and double-man handsaws, and log picks. He would have had no lack of weapons.

If he had used something from his museum, that was one set of crime scene photos I didn't want to see.

Anderson probably wasn't going to be able to win this case. If I were staying on as Clement's lawyer, I'd be talking to him about taking a plea bargain if the police arrested him for the murder. Based on his appearance, I had no doubt they would.

I made sure Troy was far enough away that he wouldn't overhear us, and then took a seat on another stump chair next to Clement.

"They're coming to talk to you next. I know you're not sure what happened, but I need you to tell me what you think went on."

His forehead was moist, and a bead of sweat drizzled its way down his temple and neck to his shirt collar. His collar was darker than the rest of his shirt, like that drizzle of sweat hadn't been the first. "I haven't been sleeping much. Almost six months now. The specialists think it's sporadic fatal insomnia. They've given me a year. Eighteen months at best."

My mouth felt like someone had stitched it shut. I'd never had anyone tell me they were dying before.

When we first met, I thought he hadn't looked well. His skin had a yellow-gray tint, and he had deep purple smears on the inside of his bloodshot eyes. His whole face had a sagging quality. Because he'd often stop in the middle of his sentences and then start up again, I'd suspected micro-seizures. I knew exhaustion could also harm a person's physical and mental health, but I hadn't known a condition called fatal insomnia even existed.

It was a good bet that if I didn't know about it, the police didn't either. The pertinent question at the moment was how his condition had played into the problem he now found himself in. "Is that why you can't remember what happened?"

"Sort of. I've been struggling with increasing paranoia and panic attacks for months now. The doctors said the next stage would be hallucinations. Last night..."

His words trailed off, and he swallowed multiple times, as if trying to grab back his escaping thoughts. I waited the same way I had when he'd taken me around his museum, though now with a greater understanding of what was behind it. It hurt something deep inside to see such a bright mind wasting away.

He blinked rapidly. "Last night, I was in my armchair, trying to read and hoping to fall asleep for a few minutes before the sun came up. The next thing I remember is a bear coming through the door and rushing me. I grabbed the closest thing I could and fought back." He shook his head. "Then my wife was screaming, and Gordon was on the floor, covered in blood."

It was a good thing I was already sitting down. My legs wouldn't have held me up, and falling on my backside wouldn't have been remotely professional.

Gordon's murder could have been staged, and Clement could have been framed. But the odds of that being the case seemed extremely remote.

Clement tugged on his Grizzly Adams beard. His rapid blinks accelerated.

I leaned back slightly on my chair. He was trying not to cry. He was afraid that he'd done this, not only because it meant he'd killed someone, but also because it meant his disease had progressed. He could see the end of his life, and it wouldn't be peaceful. It'd be filled with fear until his sanity was gone, and he wouldn't be able to escape it even in sleep.

My throat tightened. I'd once thought freezing to death would be the worst way to die. I'd been wrong.

I'd get him through the next few hours, and then I'd help him transition smoothly to Anderson. Clement needed someone who could argue on his behalf if he wanted to take this to trial. He wouldn't ever see prison time even if he was found guilty. He didn't have enough time left on his life, and his last days would be spent in a hospital as his body shut down.

The best possible outcome seemed to be to try to allow him to spend what good days he might have left in his own home. Taking this to trial, even if he thought he could be guilty, would be the way to do that. I just couldn't be the one to help him achieve that goal. He'd be found guilty for sure if I tried to argue his case in court. I could make sure he had a good lawyer in Anderson.

Movement caught my attention, and I glanced up. Chief McTavish came out the side door of the house, followed by a crime scene tech carrying a large brown object in an extra-large evidence bag.

It looked suspiciously like... "Is that my bucket?"

3

*C*hief McTavish ordered Clement brought down to the station. As they led him past the house, his wife stood off to one side with Officer Quincey Dornbush. Quincey touched the brim of his hat and gave me a little smile. Clement's wife wouldn't even look at him.

I couldn't decide whether this would be harder on Clement or on her. She'd now be afraid of her husband, and yet, if they'd had any kind of a good marriage, she probably felt terrible for telling the police what she'd seen. I knew how I'd feel if Mark was implicated in a murder and all the evidence pointed to him. That would put the strongest relationship to the test. I could only hope I never had to find out what I'd do.

At the station, while they had Clement sequestered to bag his clothes and collect evidence off his body, I ran a search on my phone for sporadic fatal insomnia. It was definitely a real thing. It was also extremely rare, caused by a mutated protein. Only about a hundred people worldwide had it.

Based on what Clement had described, he was in stage two of five, which was where hallucinations and panic attacks started to be noticeable to others. There was no known cure for fatal insomnia. There wasn't even a useful treatment. In seventy-five percent of cases, sleeping pills actually made the condition worse, so most specialists refused to prescribe them.

There wasn't much information available, but I read everything I could find until Chief McTavish called me in.

Clement wanted to tell Chief McTavish that he didn't know what had happened. While it would have been the truth, it was practically a cliché, and it would have made Chief McTavish more certain he was guilty. Telling him about the dream would have been even worse. I believed Clement, but it sounded like a crazy lie.

Instead, I convinced Clement to sit quietly and let me do the talking.

"Your wife is willing to testify against you." Chief McTavish, as expected, addressed Clement.

A lawyer wasn't personally invested, so they couldn't be goaded. Their client could. McTavish was a good officer, and he knew how to focus on the weakest link, and the spot where his suspect would be most vulnerable.

"What does that say to you?" McTavish asked.

If we hadn't been dealing with a murder, I would have called it cruel. But McTavish was only doing his job the same way I was. As much as I disliked it, I couldn't hold it against him. The quicker the police found the truth, the quicker they could eliminate suspects and arrest the real killer.

Thankfully, it'd only be my job until I could turn the case over to Anderson, and all I had to do was not screw it up too badly for him.

I stretched a hand toward Clement to remind him not to answer, no matter how much it felt like McTavish was scooping his heart out with a spoon. "It says that the Dodds are law-abiding people who want to help."

McTavish gave a slow nice-try head shake. "To me, it says he's guilty, and his wife knows it. She saw him standing over the body."

"But she didn't see him kill the victim."

"Look." Chief McTavish made sure to catch Clement's gaze and mine before continuing. "This case isn't complicated. If the blood on Mr. Dodd comes back as a match for Gordon Albright, I'll be making the arrest for Albright's murder. There are no other possible suspects here. We have a witness who came upon the scene moments after the crime. I'm too busy to waste time arguing in circles, so this is your last chance. If he confesses now, I'll speak to the DA about not asking for the harshest penalty the way he otherwise would given the brutality of the attack."

Clement leaned toward me. "If I did this, I should be locked away," he whispered.

It was the *if* that made me hesitate. I wasn't comfortable giving up and letting them book him for a crime he didn't remember committing, especially considering how short his life expectancy was. Going to trial would buy us time.

I shifted so that I could speak directly into Clement's ear. "If you did this, you should be in a mental health facility or a hospital, not in prison. First, we need to be sure you're the one responsible."

Besides, the police always made a case seem more solid than it usually was.

I folded my hands on top of the table. "Hypothetically, let's assume my client did kill Gordon Albright. It still isn't murder. Michigan has the castle doctrine. There's no duty to retreat before using deadly force on an intruder in your own home. Gordon Albright was in the Dodds' home, in the dark. He didn't live there. If my client woke up to see an intruder, he was within his legal right to act to defend himself."

Clement twitched beside me. Chief McTavish's gaze dipped in his direction. He'd spotted it too.

And I could think of only one thing it could mean. Gordon Albright wasn't an intruder in their home. He'd been invited.

"You're welcome to argue that in the preliminary hearing," Chief McTavish said, "but I think I like our chances."

ever make assumptions, my dad always said. *It'll end in you looking the fool.*

I'm sure if Anderson had already been on the case, he wouldn't have made the same mistake. I'd grown up with my dad and been trained by my dad, but Anderson practically wanted to be him.

Both of them would be shaking their heads in dismay at me now.

The police could hold a person for up to twenty-four hours before they had to either charge them with a crime or release them. Chief McTavish made it clear he planned to detain Clement, and that if they didn't have the blood results back by tomorrow, he'd apply to have the hold extended due to the severity of the crime.

Before Chief McTavish took Clement to the holding cells, I insisted on a minute alone with him and confirmed what I already knew. Gordon had been invited. Apparently, he came every morning at that time for breakfast. Chief McTavish would know it too as soon as he asked Clement's wife, and then the castle defense would be null.

Since Anderson hadn't called me back, I tried his office as soon as I reached my car. His receptionist told me he was in court all day. Given that it was only noon, I couldn't wait around the police station to introduce him to Clement. I'd have to wait to pass the case over.

Which meant I should go back to Sugarwood. I'd had a full day of work ahead of me before Clement called. Nancy and I were supposed to be packaging up the maple syrup lollipops molded in the shape of maple leafs for a wedding consignment order. Then Nancy and Stacey had asked to meet with me about expanding our product line. Even though Stacey was supposed to be on maternity leave and still hadn't told me if she planned to stay on at Sugarwood afterward, she and Nancy had all kinds of ideas about maple nougats and maple syrup fruit spreads and maple syrup truffles. Nancy promised to provide me with tasting samples.

I pulled my car out onto the road. I dug around inside myself, trying to find the same excitement for working at Sugarwood that I heard when Nancy and Stacey talked—the same excitement I'd felt driving up to the museum this morning. All I felt when thinking about a day of logistical and product meetings was tired.

Then again, if I couldn't find a way to practice as a lawyer without failing my clients in court, I might end up working at Sugarwood for the rest of my days. Maybe it wouldn't be so bad. I did enjoy testing the maple syrup products. I definitely enjoyed traipsing around the woods, which was good considering I needed the exercise after testing the maple syrup products.

And if Stacey turned down the assistant manager position and Russ' health failed, I'd have no choice.

The memory of Russ struggling to breathe turned my stomach into a heavy ball that felt too big for the space my body had to hold it.

Since he didn't have any family, we'd talked about him needing to choose someone who'd be able to help him and make decisions for him as he aged. I hadn't realized when I brought it up that I'd be the one he asked. Right now, all that meant was that I was on file at the pharmacy as being allowed to pick up medications and speak to the pharmacist on his behalf. I'd picked up his high blood pressure medication before when I was running errands.

Even though Russ hadn't asked me to pick anything up this time, I had to do something. If he wasn't taking a newly prescribed medication, he was putting himself at greater risk. I couldn't make him take it. I couldn't make him take better care of himself. But I wouldn't sit by and watch him slowly kill himself, either.

Sugarwood business could wait an extra ten minutes.

I took a left at the next light instead of going right to head back to Sugarwood. I'd just swing by the pharmacy and make sure Russ had picked up any medications his doctor called in.

Like most businesses in Fair Haven, the pharmacy wasn't part of a big chain. The large red-and-white sign on the front of the building carried the name DR. HORTON'S DRUG STORE.

Also, like most businesses in Fair Haven that catered to locals rather than tourists, it didn't have a cutesy name. I did know now, though, that the owner not only wasn't a doctor, his name also wasn't Horton. It was an inside joke for the locals. Horton was a character in the children's book *Horton Hears a Who* by Dr. Seuss, who also hadn't been a doctor at all. The owner's real name was Victor Kristoffersen—a last name so long it wouldn't have fit on the small sign even if he had wanted to use it.

I entered the store. Saul Emmitt, the pharmacist, was the only one behind the pharmacy counter, as usual. Last spring, when he'd needed major reconstructive back surgery, he hadn't even taken the full medical leave of absence his doctor recommended. Mr. Kristoffersen himself filled in for a couple of weeks despite being semi-retired, but I suspected that Saul was his only employee. Dr. Horton's even closed on the weekends, which was something I still hadn't adapted to, coming from a city where many pharmacies stayed open 24/7.

Saul drove his electric wheelchair out and around the counter. He'd started doing that after the failed surgery left him mostly paralyzed. If I'd had to guess, I would have said that he didn't like feeling hidden and small. He hadn't specifically told me that, but he had mentioned casually at one point that, when Mr. Kristoffersen finally decided to sell him the business, the first thing he planned to do was remodel the store to drop the counters down. He didn't want to spend the next fifteen to twenty years of his working life dealing with counters that were too high for a man in a wheelchair.

"Nice to see you again, Nicole. Are you dropping off or picking up?"

"Picking up." The words stuck a little in my throat. Hopefully Russ wouldn't be too angry at me. "For Russ."

He wheeled back around. "Something did come in almost a

week ago now. I left a couple messages for Russ. I was starting to worry his number had changed."

My suspicions had been right, then. His doctor prescribed him something new, and he was avoiding it, either because of the cost or because Russ was a bit of a hypochondriac who was more afraid of the side effects of medication than of the condition the medication was meant to treat.

Saul bent forward to look through the drawers of prescriptions ready for pick-up, and his head disappeared from view. "I hear you decided to stay in Fair Haven rather than moving back to DC," his disembodied voice said.

If I wasn't certain it was impossible, I would have thought Fair Haven residents were telepathic with how effectively they were able to spread news. "We did. It was a joint decision between Mark and me."

"What do you plan to do here for a job?"

It was an innocent enough question, but I'd been personally wresting with it for so long that, whenever someone else asked, it felt almost accusatory, like they thought I was either going to go on unemployment when I should be working or I was going to steal a job from a local who didn't have other options. Most people who asked didn't mean either of those things. In fact, most people who asked saw me as a local now and hadn't wanted me to leave Fair Haven. I still felt censure in the question because it seemed like I should have it figured out by now.

Saul straightened up, a white bag in his hand. He set it in his lap. I must have hesitated too long in answering because the look he gave me said he realized it wasn't as simple a question as it seemed.

"Small towns tend to be nosy. If gossip were an Olympic sport, we'd take the gold. You don't have to feel pressured to tell me anything you don't want to." He tilted his head to the side. "Though if you're prescribed a new medication, I would recommend you tell me about any other medication, vitamins, or herbal supplements you might be on."

I chuckled. I hadn't consciously thought about it, but once he acknowledged the small town your-business-*is*-my-business mentality, I couldn't help wondering if part of my reticence to discuss it with anyone was that whatever I said would find its way around Fair Haven before I even got home. I could count the number of people I'd confided in on one hand.

Dr. Horton's was a bit of a community hub. In the summer, I'd passed by no fewer than four retirees sitting at the patio tables on the sidewalk out front, gossiping and drinking coffee. Saul probably knew more about what went on in this town than almost anyone else, but he seemed more like a bartender who heard it all but kept it to himself. At least, he'd never discussed anyone else's business with me when I came in. Maybe as a pharmacist, he had a greater respect for privacy.

He held out the bag. "I'll go over the instructions and side effects with you, but would you let me give you a piece of advice first?"

The fact that he bothered to ask won my approval. I nodded.

"If you can do the career you love, you should. Too many people never get that chance." He pointed with one finger over his shoulder, toward his back. He smiled, but it was the kind people gave when they hoped it would cover up what they were really feeling. "I didn't."

As long as I'd been in Fair Haven, Saul had always worn a back brace and walked with a walker, even before he'd ended up in a wheelchair. He'd also always seemed to enjoy his job. I hadn't considered that his life had ever been radically different or that he'd once wanted to do something else.

Most people probably didn't know how much he still wished he had been able to do that something else. He was a master at small town living. He'd learned how to truly hide what he didn't want anyone else to know. I bet I wasn't the only one he'd managed to fool.

I was a good actress when it came to dealing with witnesses and potential suspects, but I couldn't maintain a mask like that for the rest of my life.

More than that, I didn't want to. "I'm considering going back to practicing law. It's what I did in DC. But there are...obstacles."

"All I'm saying is make sure you do whatever it takes to have no regrets one day," Saul said.

He'd hit on exactly what worried me most. Before I gave up on a career as a defense lawyer, I needed to either find a way to make my career as a lawyer work, or I needed to find a way to learn to love working at Sugarwood just as much as I loved practicing law.

Right now, both seemed about as likely as finding a unicorn roaming my sugar bush.

5

*F*or the rest of the day and most of the next, I kept expecting to hear from Chief McTavish that he'd charged Clement with Gordon Albright's murder. Even while I was eating the maple syrup nougat and maple syrup truffles Nancy had created for us to start selling online, and even while I was holding my little godson Noah, my mind kept drifting back to Clement's case.

I was out in the bush with Russ, overseeing the yearly clean-up of underbrush, fallen branches, and downed trees, when my phone rang. I immediately stopped moving. There was a reason we used old-fashioned walkie-talkies when working in the sugar bush. Cell phone signals were sporadic and unreliable. If this was Chief McTavish calling to tell me they'd arrested Clement, I didn't want to miss the call.

It was Anderson's number on my screen.

"I hear you're trying to muscle in on my business." His tone started out serious, but he couldn't hold it together. By the end of the sentence, it was clear he was teasing.

"That might be true if I wanted to keep the case. You should be paying me a commission for finding you a new client."

"What's the case?" he said, all jocularity gone from his voice.

I filled him in.

He whistled. "I heard about a murder at the museum on the radio. They hadn't released the victim's name yet. Are you thinking he's lying about not knowing what happened?"

I didn't. As crazy as his story sounded, I believed Clement. He seemed genuinely confused and distraught. Plus, he'd have no reason to lie to me about his guilt or innocence. Confidentiality guaranteed he could tell me exactly how he'd plotted to kill Gordon and then how he'd carried it out, and I wouldn't be able to tell anyone about it.

The only reason I could tell Anderson was that we'd signed a consultancy agreement so that he could pick my brain on cases without violating his own client's confidentiality. There'd been language in it that allowed me to do the same. I hadn't thought I'd need to exercise the option so soon.

"I read up on his medical condition a little, and I think he's telling the truth."

"Then I don't understand why you want to pass this case along to me. He seems like exactly the kind of client you're willing to defend. If he turns out to be guilty, he'll want to plead out."

Maybe the cases I worked could be more varied than I thought. While it wasn't common, sometimes people who'd committed a crime did want to confess. I could help those people as well because they weren't trying to hide their crime. Like Bonnie, Toby's original owner. I'd negotiated a fair plea deal for her, and I visited her every month. I even brought her pictures of Toby.

If Clement was willing to make a deal if it turned out he was guilty, then there wasn't an ethical or moral reason I couldn't represent him.

"And," Anderson said, "my case load is packed. I can't take on another client right now. I'm already working evenings and weekends. I don't even have time to interview candidates for adding another lawyer to the firm."

I didn't want to hand Clement over to a stranger. Most lawyers would think he was lying. Anderson probably only believed his story because I said I did. "If this goes to trial, with all the evidence against him, he'll need a lawyer who's great in the courtroom. That's not me."

"Since we were both students of your dad, I'm going to consider myself your professional brother and give you some tough love. If you want to be in this career, you have to overcome your problems in the courtroom."

This felt eerily familiar to the discussion I'd had with Elise when she wanted me to represent her ex-husband. I'd managed to figure out what happened in that case before I had to go into a courtroom. That wouldn't always be possible.

By the wood pile, Russ was sitting on a log, directing the workers. I'd never seen him sit like a foreman rather than working alongside everyone else before. Maybe I should give up the whole lawyer thing and simply take over from Russ. Stacey still wasn't sure whether she wanted to take the position as assistant manager or not. In fact, she seemed to be actively avoiding the conversation, which made me nervous.

Saul's words came back to me. *If you can do the career you love, you should. Too many people never get that chance.*

Taking back the duties that Stacey had been handling had shown me how much I didn't enjoy processing orders and doing payroll. I loved being a lawyer. I didn't want to reach the end of my life and look back and wonder if I could have done it if I'd tried harder or hadn't given up so soon.

Anderson and I had also talked casually about me joining his firm as a partner rather than launching my own. He understood that I'd only be willing to work specific cases, but he'd felt that having the Fitzhenry-Dawes name would be a fair tradeoff.

I'd been putting him off because it didn't seem right to work a case and then hand it off to him for the trial. He'd end up doing a large portion of the work on my cases if I couldn't see them through.

But it also didn't seem fair to Clement to use him as a test case. It was a bit like learning to walk a tightrope without a net or safety harness. "I'm scared I'll screw up and he'll end up in prison because of me."

The silence on Anderson's end stretched.

My heart rate picked up to the same rate it would if I pulled out to pass a car and only then noticed another vehicle bearing down on me in the other lane. *Never show weakness,* my dad always said. *People respect strength.*

Anderson was such a devotee of my dad's that I half expected him to quote it to me.

"That's the risk we take," he said softly. "It's easy when they're guilty. It's not so easy with the ones we think are innocent."

I let out a breath I hadn't realized I was holding. I had to remember that Anderson admired my dad, but he wasn't my dad. I'd had to fight to get my dad to view me as a competent equal. Anderson gave me that respect from the start. Granted, a lot of it had been due to my name rather than my abilities, but he'd also seen my investigative and problem-solving skills now as well.

"Listen," he continued, "how about this? I'll be co-counsel with you on this case if you'd like. You take point, but if it looks like you can't handle it, I'll be there to step in. Consider me your training wheels."

---

6

*T*he call I'd been expecting from Chief McTavish finally came in as I was putting together a salad to go with the chicken penne I'd cooked for dinner with Mark. It wasn't going to be a fancy meal, but I was determined to be able to put together a few simple meals before we got married. When children came along, I didn't want to raise them entirely on fish and chips dinners from A Salt & Battery.

"The blood spatter on Dodd's clothes, skin, and hair was a match for Gordon Albright, and his wife confirmed that Albright would have been there under a standing invitation," McTavish said. "I'm waiting now on the arrest orders. It should be done tonight. I'm sorry this didn't work out the way you were hoping, but I'm confident he's our guy."

I understood. Clement looked guilty any way you turned it. This wasn't the first time I'd worked a case that seemed like there was only one possible suspect, though.

"I'll be by to talk to him tomorrow."

"I was sure you would be."

I disconnected with McTavish at the same time as Mark came through the door. The dogs rushed him with their happy wiggles, but I could have sworn Velma looked confused by his lack of take-out bags for her to try to sniff—and steal. Apparently, pasta was much less enticing than French fries because when I'd dropped a piece on the floor earlier, Velma snarfed it up and then spit it back out.

He did have a sheaf of papers with him.

I glanced at them sidelong. "What are those?"

"Pictures of flower options. My mom says you can't put it off any longer. The florist needs to know."

An unpleasant tingle ran from my shoulders to my hands. I knew I eventually had to deal with the flowers, but every time I tried, it brought back memories of my previous case. Even though it hadn't been intentional, I'd gotten a person killed because of flowers. Elise had forgiven me, but forgiving myself was turning out to be harder than I'd expected.

"We'll save the plants until after we eat, at least." Mark shrugged off his coat. "You look frustrated. Is it from making dinner? Should I have brought take-out after all?"

I swallowed down a snort. Sugarwood's resident baker Nancy, my friend Mandy, and Mark's mom had all been taking turns giving me cooking lessons. Mark and I had a for-fun wager going about which of them I'd drive to quitting first.

"I almost wish that were the case. McTavish is arresting Clement Dodd."

Mark gathered up utensils and plates while I carried the salad to the table. "I'm not surprised. You'll see it when you get the report, but it was a straightforward autopsy. Cause of death was blunt force trauma. He had defensive wounds on his hands and arms, and nothing out of the ordinary in his stomach or on the toxicology screening. You might want to consider handing the case off to someone else. Based on what I saw, Dodd is guilty."

I went back for the bowl of chicken penne and plunked it down on the table. Mark rarely drew conclusions from his autopsies. He felt his role was to present the evidence, explain his results in court, and allow the lawyers to draw arguments and conclusions from it all. For him to make a statement like that, it must really look like there wasn't another solution. And he'd seen the crime scene. I still hadn't. I wouldn't receive pictures until I got the discovery package from the prosecution.

I dropped into my chair. "I tried to pass the case off to Anderson already. He wouldn't take it."

I recounted our conversation to Mark, and then he said grace over the food before we dug in. My pasta came out a little soggy, but otherwise, it wasn't half bad.

"I think Anderson's right that you should try going to court," Mark said once he'd polished off half his plate. "This is a good case to do it on because..." He gave me a don't-get-mad look. "Even your parents couldn't win this one."

I wanted to argue with him, but unless my parents found a procedural technicality that would call for a mistrial—and with Chief McTavish in charge, I doubted there'd been one—the case did look impossible. Clement's insomnia made it unbelievable that someone else could have sneaked into the house with an already-dead Gordon Albright. And not only sneaked in. They would have had to splatter Gordon's blood all over Clement without him noticing.

"The only other person in the house was his wife. Do you think a woman would have been capable of inflicting the wounds on Gordon?"

Mark shook his head. "Not a woman of Darlene Dodd's size. She wouldn't be able to create the force needed. Albright had wood fragments from the bucket in his wounds. It was swung so hard the bucket's basically held together by the metal bands at this point."

It was stupid to mourn for my bucket when a man had lost his life, but I couldn't help it. I also couldn't help wishing for the impossible. "I don't want Clement to be guilty. He's a nice man."

"I remember you telling me how much you enjoyed meeting him the first time."

No *he might not be guilty*. No *there's always a chance*. Mark wasn't a pessimist, but he was realistic. He wouldn't want to build up false hopes in me.

Clement's apparent guilt did seem to make this the perfect test case for me. A hopeless case meant I couldn't screw it up. A client who was likely guilty but didn't want to hide his guilt and hadn't wanted to hurt anyone meant I could defend him in good conscience.

Based on what Clement told me about his medical condition and hallucinating a bear, I'd probably suggest he be evaluated by a forensic mental health professional. That evaluation should open up some possibilities for what we could argue in court even if he had done it.

I slowly chewed my last bite of chicken. "I have time to decide. The first thing we need to do is get through the bail hearing so Clement can go home."

7

*T*he next morning, when I showed up at the police station to talk to Clement about his bail hearing, Quincey led me down the hallway that went to the cells.

I'd personally spent some time in the cells last winter, and they weren't built for hosting guests. I wouldn't have anywhere to sit. "Why isn't he being brought up to an interview room to meet with me?"

"His request. It's the first time I've ever seen it happen." Quincey put an arm in front of my path before we went through the final set of doors. "There's no one else in the cells right now, so I'll wait out here to give you privacy. All you need to do is knock."

Quincey wasn't even going to unlock his cell door? That was odd to say the least. It must have been Clement's request as well. There wasn't any point in asking Quincey about it. If he hadn't known why Clement refused to meet with me in the traditional setting, he wouldn't know the reasoning behind this choice, either.

I made my way down the walkway between the cells and stopped at the first occupied one. Clement perched on the edge of his bed, elbows on his knees, his hands dangling loose. He looked up when I stopped, but he didn't immediately say anything.

I hadn't thought it was possible for Clement to look worse. I'd been wrong. He looked faded, like a black-and-white picture of himself.

I wrapped a hand around one of the bars. "How have you been?"

His shoulders hunched forward. "There's too much time to think here. At least at home, when I couldn't sleep, I'd read, or Darlene would stay up with me, and we'd play a game of chess."

"The bail review hearing is scheduled for tomorrow. You should be able to go home then. You're a well-known and respected member of the community, and you're not a flight risk. It's more a formality than anything."

The look he gave me was so empty it made me feel as if I was going to be sucked in and forget how to smile, like a black hole of unhappiness. Not that I expected Clement to be happy at all about what had happened—I'd be concerned if he was—but this was a new level of despair from when I'd seen him last time.

"I can't go home. Darlene came and saw me last night, and we talked. She's right. If I did this to Gordon, I'm a danger to others."

I'd been so focused on Clement's disease and pitying him that I hadn't thought about the wider implications of this. If Clement killed Gordon because he'd been hallucinating and thought he was a bear, his wife would be in danger. He could also be a danger to others.

"Is that why you refused to come out of your cell?"

He nodded. "I can't trust myself."

Darlene was right, but the suspicious part of me also thought that it would be a perfect way to continue framing her husband for a murder she might have committed. Mark had been certain, though, that a woman would have had a hard time doing the damage Gordon suffered. Unless Darlene had an accomplice, I could cross her off the list as an alternative way to explain what had happened.

And that brought us to the real crux of the situation.

"So what do you want from this? Most people, when they hire a defense attorney, only care about an acquittal."

"I want the truth." He ran his fingers through his beard. "Darlene and I were high school sweethearts. We were almost a cliché. Football player and cheerleader. We've been married thirty-five years. Now she's afraid of me. She hasn't looked at me the same since. Not going to prison isn't enough if I lose my best friend."

He stopped talking suddenly, like he'd forgotten where he'd been going with what he was saying. Now that I understood what was happening, I waited rather than assuming he was done.

He blinked rapidly a few times. "I already lost a good friend. Gordon was a friend to both of us. If I did this, I need to be locked up where I can't hurt anyone else. If I didn't, whoever killed him needs to be punished for it, and Darlene needs to be able to be sure that she's safe with me."

Mark had once commented that it didn't seem like finding evidence to clear a client was enough for me. I always seemed to want to find the real killer, because the truth mattered, and someone should be held accountable for causing all that pain.

Listening to Clement was like hearing my own thoughts parroted back to me.

If Clement had killed Gordon in a hallucination, we'd talk about best options. I still didn't think prison was the right place for him, but he would need to go somewhere that he couldn't hurt anyone else during a moment of delirium.

Instead of turning Clement over to Anderson as a client, I'd accept Anderson's suggestion of working this one as co-counsel. It felt like the right thing to do to see this case through. Clement wasn't trying to get away with a crime, and that's what I hadn't liked about working for my parents. And Anderson would be there to skillfully argue Clement's case if this did end up going to trial.

I moved as close to the bars as I could so that he could clearly see my face. "I'll find the truth for you. I promise."

_a_s soon as I was out of the police station, I called Darlene Dodd and asked if she had time to speak with me. She told me to meet her at their house. The police had released the scene, and she'd already hired a crime scene clean-up crew to deal with the mess.

My mind gnawed on that as I drove. The suspicious part of me wondered about how fast she'd moved, as if she didn't want me getting a look at the scene before the evidence was gone. The rational part of me knew I wouldn't have waited an additional minute once the police cleared the scene to have it cleaned up, either. There'd be no way to process what had happened and start to cope as long as blood coated your house. Besides, the police would have taken plenty of pictures that I would look over.

Darlene waited for me outside the house when I pulled up. I hadn't paid much attention to her the day of the murder. Today she wore jeans and an oversized fuzzy green-and-black coat that looked like it might belong to Clement, given the size. Her blonde hair was naturally curly and almost as wide as her face was tall. She reminded me a little bit of a younger Kate Chapshaw.

Darlene hugged her coat around herself even though the zipper was done up. "I thought I'd meet you out here. We can either talk in the kitchen or the living room, your choice."

She turned her statement into a question somehow, like she lacked the self-confidence to choose for herself where it would be best for us to talk.

I'd made the assumption because Clement said he'd been trying to fall asleep in his chair that he'd been in the living room. The crime scene clean-up crew's truck was still here, though. "Won't we be in the way in the living room?"

She shook her head, opened her mouth, and closed it again like she was searching for words. "It happened in Clem's office."

That was a bit odd. And bad for our case. If someone brought Gordon's body in, the most logical place to plant him was the living room. They wouldn't know which room the office was or where it was or how often it was used unless they were intimately familiar with the family.

"Did Gordon usually go into Clement's office when he came over for breakfast?"

Her smile looked stiff around the edges like old leather. "Always. They were the ones who cooked. Even before he stopped sleeping, Clem was the early riser. I hate mornings. Clem came to wake me when breakfast was ready. Gordon makes...made the best blueberry waffles you ever tasted."

She had the red around the nose and eyes of someone who'd

spent much of the previous day crying, but her eyes were dry now. That struck me as authentic. If she'd been wanting to convince me of grief she didn't feel, she'd have been blubbering. She wasn't. She was trying to hold strong.

Even if Mark hadn't said a woman probably couldn't have done that amount of damage to Gordon, I wouldn't have believed Darlene was responsible now. Her grief was too genuine, and I didn't detect any signs of underlying guilt. She met my gaze, albeit in a shy way, and her responses sounded matter-of-fact. Sad, but matter-of-fact.

I didn't usually believe in *innocent until proven guilty* when it came to potential suspects, but in this case, that's how I was going to approach it.

A cold gust of wind lifted my hair and Darlene's. She touched my arm. "Why don't we go inside? I'm sure you have questions, or you wouldn't be here."

She took my coat once we were inside and hung her own up as well. Her shoulders were slightly too broad for her hips, giving her a top-heavy look. Clement mentioned that she was a cheerleader. With her strong shoulders, she'd probably been one of the girls on the bottom of the pyramid.

I accepted her offer of coffee. She left me in the living room. Through the far wall, I could hear muffled voices, presumably the clean-up crew. That was a job I definitely wouldn't want. Seeing blood in pictures was bad enough. The less blood I could see in real life, the better.

A chess set that looked like it was made from marble rested on a table in the corner, and a red brick fireplace ate up a third of their

living room's far wall. Pictures filled the mantel. Darlene's temporary absence gave me a good opportunity to poke around a little and
get a better idea of their life.

In the place of honor, where I'd have expected to find their
wedding photo, was a picture of a boy of about ten, holding up a
fish that was nearly as long as his entire torso. His square face and
glasses reminded me of a little Clement, but it couldn't be Clement
as a boy. The picture was too recent. Not taken on a digital camera
or phone by any means, but at least into the era of photography
where the colors were bright and the image was clear.

To the right was a picture of a clean-shaven Clement in a graduation gown and Darlene in a dress with unflattering shoulder pads,
holding a baby. It looked like Clement got his college degree while
Darlene stayed home. The baby was probably the boy in the photo
with the fish. It must be their son. Hopefully they'd called him to tell
him what was going on. Some people thought it was better to hide
bad news from their children.

To the far left was a picture of a high school football team. I
leaned closer and studied the faces until I found Clement. If I hadn't
seen the graduation photo first, I wouldn't have recognized him.
The beard he wore now changed his look dramatically.

It must be the Fair Haven high school team. A few of the other
faces were ones I knew as well—Stacey's dad Tony Rathmell, the
Fair Haven police force dispatcher, my pharmacist Saul Emmitt, and
the head of the construction crew that rebuilt my historical-replica
sugar shack. Based on what Saul said earlier, I'd thought he might
have been born with spinal issues, but it looked like he'd been at
least able to manage throughout high school.

It made me feel even more than I had before that I should listen to his advice. In high school, I'd assumed I'd be a first-class lawyer the way my parents were. My parents weren't the only ones who were disappointed when it looked like I hadn't inherited their abilities in the courtroom.

Gordon wasn't in the team photo, but he was in one on the other side. Gordon and Clement stood out in the middle of the woods, shotguns beside them. Of course he had to be a hunter. My dad hated defending people who hunted because many jurors had a subconscious bias that people who killed animals for sport were more likely to kill people, too. Hopefully we could keep that from coming out.

"I don't ever make coffee," Darlene pushed open the door with her shoulder, "so I hope this is drinkable. Clement usually makes our pot of morning coffee."

I'd drunk enough cups of Mandy's strong-enough-to-clean-your-grout coffee that I was sure I could choke down anything now.

I moved away from the mantel and took a chair across from Darlene.

She balanced her mug on her knee, her fingers hooked around the handle just enough to steady it. Her gaze strayed to the office door, but with an I'm-out-of-my-depth look. My instincts said that Clement had probably used his one phone call to hire the clean-up crew rather than that Darlene had hired them. Clement seemed to be the one who handled most things.

Based on that, maybe the best thing I could do to help her through this would be to let her know she didn't have to handle it alone.

"Part of my role is to make sure you and Clement have an ally and an advocate every step of the way, not only to defend him, but to make sure everything is taken care of and to answer your questions." I inclined my head toward the mantle. "Have you called your son to let him know? It's often helpful if the family is in court showing support for the accused, and it might make it easier for you to have someone around the house for a few days."

Darlene's gaze darted to the mantle and her cup tilted. She righted it at the last minute. "I guess you wouldn't know. Our son drowned in a fishing accident shortly after that picture was taken."

Great. I'd managed to make it worse for her, not better, by reminding her of her dead child. My voice didn't want to work, which wasn't surprising considering I had my foot in my mouth. I cleared my throat. "Is there anything you'd like to ask me about the case?"

Darlene swiveled the cup back and forth on her knee. "Can they make me testify against Clement?"

Darlene believed Clement was guilty. He'd said as much when I talked to him earlier, and I could see it in her every movement now. That put her in a terrible position. She loved her husband and didn't want to feel like she was betraying him. But it looked like he'd murdered their friend.

More than anything, I wanted to fix that for them by proving someone else killed Gordon.

"The law protects the spousal relationship. They can't make you testify against Clement if you don't want to."

"I don't want to," she said quietly.

I opened my mouth to tell her that I planned to do my best to prove him innocent, not only in the eyes of the law, but also in her eyes as well.

I snapped my mouth back shut before the words spilled out. I couldn't guarantee anything, and the last thing this woman needed was potentially false hope. Especially given my misstep a minute ago about their son.

I sipped my coffee to buy myself a few seconds to reorganize my thoughts. I needed to figure out how to make her understand that we were all in agreement, but to also make sure she knew how important the information she gave me would be. And I had to do it in a noncommittal way so she wasn't crushed if what I found out was that Clement was as guilty as Jack the Ripper.

I set aside my coffee and pulled out my notepad and pen. "If we're going to keep you off the stand, I need to make sure I know everything useful to Clement's defense and have alternate ways to bring it in. I'll need you to answer a few questions for me now. Who would have known Gordon came over every morning at that time for breakfast?"

She did a headshake-shrug combo. "It wasn't a secret, but I don't think anyone specifically knew it was every morning that he came."

Someone still could have known about it through the Fair Haven gossip system and decided to frame Clement. Since Gordon had a habit of coming, it wouldn't have been a sound defense for Clement to claim that particular morning wasn't one when he'd been invited.

"Do you keep your doors locked?"

"It's a small town."

In other words, no. At least I wasn't surprised. Russ didn't lock his doors, either. It drove me batty, especially when he'd come into my house and leave without locking the door.

Unlocked doors meant we couldn't even narrow down possibilities. "Can you think of anyone who might have wanted to hurt Gordon?"

Darlene switched her mug from one knee to the other and frowned. "Why does this matter? Clement doesn't want you trying to prove he didn't do something he did."

I chewed the inside of my cheek. That was her first evasive answer. Darlene was still meeting my gaze, and her answers weren't too rushed or too slow. She didn't seem flushed or sweaty. She wasn't showing any of the signs I would have expected from someone who was lying to me or had something to hide. She could be a psychopath or a sociopath, but that didn't fit with the way she chose to show emotions in private and hide them in front of me. A psychopath would manufacture emotions when someone was watching.

So what was going on here? What was I missing? Maybe she didn't believe Clement's story about seeing a bear and suspected that he'd planned Gordon's murder.

"Did Clement have a reason to want to kill Gordon?" I asked.

"No. And I did tell the police that."

If she gave the same vibe to the police as I was getting now, the police would have probably suspected the same thing. I could hear my mom's teaching prompting me to be a little firmer with her. As much as I hated it, this time I agreed. "You don't want to testify against Clement, but you don't seem to want to help him, either."

She glanced at the door that must lead into the office where the clean-up crew was working. "I love Clement. I've loved him since I was fifteen years old. But I didn't know the man who was standing over Gordon."

Her voice took on a scratchy quality.

This I'd seen before. After a tragedy, human nature seemed to be to vocalize one's confusion. You heard it anytime the neighbors or family of a murderer were interviewed. *I just don't understand it,* they'd say. They'd say it to the police. They'd say it to the press. They'd say it to each other. And what I was coming to realize more and more was that, even when a motive was revealed, they'd keep saying it for the rest of their lives, because none of us liked to think we could be deceived about the character of the people we knew.

Darlene's chest rose and fell rapidly, and her body had tensed throughout her speech. People couldn't smell fear, but I could almost feel her fear coming off of her. And I could hear what she hadn't said. She loved Clement, but she no longer felt safe with him. She no longer trusted that he wouldn't hurt her or someone else because Gordon had been a long-time friend to them both. If Clement would kill him, seemingly randomly, then he could do the same to anyone.

She felt like I wouldn't care about that. Defense attorneys didn't have the best reputations, even in small towns. If we were going to make progress, I had to rectify that.

"Clement made it clear to me that, if he did kill Gordon, he wants to make sure he's put someplace where he can't hurt anyone else. I'm going to fulfill his wishes. Since he can't remember what happened, though, I want to make sure we have all the facts first. Is there anyone else who might have wanted to kill Gordon?"

She sucked her bottom lip into her mouth for a moment. "Gordon and his brother hadn't talked to each other since their mother died. That's the only person I can think of. And his brother's the only person I can think of who knew for sure Gordon came here for breakfast every morning."

9

*C*onsidering how my assumptions got me into trouble during Clement's interview with Chief McTavish, I wasn't going to make a similar mistake and walk into a meeting with Gordon's brother without some sense of direction. Besides, not speaking to a sibling didn't necessarily mean you'd want to murder that sibling. My dad and Uncle Stan were the perfect example. They hadn't spoken in years, and yet my dad wouldn't have killed Uncle Stan.

Even though Gordon's brother looked like my best option for finding someone who might have had a reason to kill Gordon, it was still a long shot, and I needed more information.

I started to dial the number for Hal, the private investigator I'd used to help dig up information during my last case, but stopped before I'd finished entering his number. On that case, I'd been working solo, so I paid Hal myself. This time, I was technically working with Anderson. We hadn't discussed specifics for invoicing contractors.

I deleted Hal's number and entered Anderson's instead. When he answered, I explained what I'd learned so far and asked about the procedure for hiring Hal.

"At first I thought you were going to want me to join you when you met with the victim's brother."

I hadn't gotten that far in my thinking, but it wasn't a bad idea. Chances were Gordon's brother was innocent. But chances also were that six separate criminals wouldn't attempt to kill the same person in the span of a year, and I'd proven those odds wrong. I didn't take chances anymore.

"I would like you to come along. My dad always felt two lawyers should attend every interview. Extra perspective."

Anderson sighed. "That's another reason I need to hire an extra lawyer."

My rescuer soul wanted to rush in to fill that need, but I caught the words in time. Even if I accepted his partnership offer, I wouldn't be working cases on guilty clients. He'd still need at least one other lawyer in the firm.

"I can work it into my schedule to join you," Anderson said, "but we're on our own for research this week. Hal's on vacation."

Talk about inconvenient timing.

I thanked Anderson and told him I'd text him with a couple potential appointment times.

By the time we disconnected, I was back at Sugarwood.

The note tacked to my door told me Mandy had taken my dogs

for a walk. I appreciated her thoughtfulness to leave the note. After the events of a few months ago, I'd been extra nervous if I came home and found them gone. Thankfully, Mandy had loaded the app onto my phone that let me track Velma through the GPS in her collar. I clicked over to the app, and it showed Velma out in the sugar bush, exactly where she should be if Mandy had them out for a walk.

I didn't think I'd made anyone involved in the current case nervous enough to mess with my dogs, but I also didn't know for sure. If Clement hadn't killed Gordon, then the real killer could be almost anyone. For all I knew, Darlene had a lover and they'd killed Gordon together.

The thought that perhaps Gordon's brother and Darlene were having an affair flitted across my mind. Gordon could have found out and threatened to tell Clement. That would be another plausible reason for why Darlene hadn't wanted to tell me that Gordon and his brother weren't speaking.

It's also completely unfounded, my dad's voice chimed in my head.

Unfounded for now, I thought back.

Though an affair with Gordon's brother didn't match up at all for why the brothers stopped speaking after their mom died. I probably was on the wrong track with that idea.

I flipped open my laptop and ran an Internet search for Gordon and Leonard Albright. Darlene hadn't told me their mother's name, but looking for both the brothers together should give me something.

The top result was an obituary for a Maryanne Albright. Gordon and Leonard were listed among the family she left behind. It looked like they'd been her only children, and her husband predeceased her. Leonard was married and had given his mother two grandchildren. Maryanne had been another casualty of cancer. It seemed like no one was untouched by it anymore. Even if they hadn't had it themselves, they had a friend or family member who had.

An obituary wasn't going to tell me why the woman's children weren't speaking anymore. I went back to the results page.

I flipped through the next three pages of results. None of them were pertinent. The only other one that even referenced the right Gordon Albright was a newspaper article about the opening of a new exhibit at the museum.

The picture that went along with it showed Gordon, Clement, and Darlene out front of the museum. Darlene held up an axe, and Clement and Gordon each held the end of one of those long dual-man saws. Since Gordon hadn't been killed with either an axe or a saw, that article wasn't helpful either.

I read it over quickly anyway. It did add a little background I hadn't known about Clement. It turned out he'd gone to university on a full-ride football scholarship. He'd had a few NFL teams interested in him when he graduated, but he turned down a career in sports and instead worked at various large museums across the country until five years ago.

His dad passed away and left him the chainsaw and logging museum, which at the time was nothing more than an extension built on their house. Clement and Darlene, apparently with the help of Gordon, built the museum up into one of the premier logging museums in the country.

I hadn't realized there were other chainsaw and logging museums in the country.

Unless Clement killed Gordon with premeditation because Gordon was stealing and selling their museum pieces, the article wasn't that helpful, either. I wrote the idea down just in case the prosecution tried to use it. I'd make sure with Darlene and Clement that nothing had gone missing.

I rubbed at my eyes with the heels of my hands to help them refocus. Another cup of coffee would taste amazing right about now, but I'd discovered that I slept better if I avoided coffee after three in the afternoon. Considering that one of my biggest challenges was convincing my mind to shut down enough at night to allow me to sleep, I didn't want to mess with what seemed to be working. And I hated decaf. It tasted like chemicals.

I chugged a glass of water instead and returned to my computer.

Unfortunately, I wasn't used to handling the background checks involved in an investigation myself. My parents had investigators who did this, and I'd worked with Hal or the police here in Fair Haven. I wasn't sure of all the avenues to chase to see what dark secrets the brothers might have been hiding.

The only other thing I could think of was to run a credit check on both of them and to put their names into the online legal records search. I logged into the system and entered Gordon's name.

It popped up immediately. A civil suit involving Gordon Albright and Leonard Albright. Leonard had alleged that Gordon misused his power of attorney for property to take their mother's money and use it for himself, draining all her accounts so that nothing remained of the estate upon her death.

My mouth went dry in a way that water wouldn't help. Maybe my long shot wasn't such a long shot after all. Depending on how much money Leonard thought he should have inherited from their mother upon her death, that could be a motive to not only stop speaking to his brother, but to kill him as well.

"WHAT DID YOU TELL HIM ABOUT WHY WE WANTED TO MEET WITH him?" Anderson asked from the passenger seat of my car a few days later as we drove to our appointment with Leonard Albright.

"The truth, of course."

The look Anderson gave me said *Are you sure you're really your father's daughter?* "You told him we were coming because we want to know if he's the one who really killed his brother."

"I told him we believe Clement is innocent, and we want to talk to him about whether there's anyone else who might have wanted to hurt Gordon."

Anderson smirked at me and shook his head. "I'm not sure I'd call that truth. I've looked at the evidence. You're the only one who thinks there's a chance Clement Dodd didn't kill Gordon Albright."

It wasn't so much that I thought Clement was innocent as I'd seen cases that looked airtight burst a leak when you stomped on them hard enough. But I wasn't interested in arguing that point right now. "Why did you come with me, then, if you don't think there's a chance Clement's innocent? My dad would say it's a waste of company resources."

"Aren't you the one who once told me your dad's not always right?" He shrugged. "It's what partners do. If you think this is important to your case, I'll back you on it. Worse case, the brothers' broken relationship helps us establish reasonable doubt."

His words created a warm little buzz in the part of my brain where my confidence liked to hide. His I've-got-your-back attitude was why I was even considering joining his firm as a partner. He knew I'd be chasing what looked like rabbit trails to defend innocent clients, and he was okay with it.

When we'd first started talking about it, I'd asked him why. He'd said it was because he wanted his firm to find its own niche. He didn't want to be just another lawyer trying to topple Edward Dawes from his throne.

Anderson had gone quiet in the passenger's seat, reading over the printout of the lawsuit I'd found. "You did see that Leonard dropped the suit, didn't you?"

I nodded. "Dropping the suit actually raised more questions for me. He wouldn't have filed a suit against his brother if he hadn't been convinced of his wrongdoing. If he'd been merely suspicious, he likely would have spoken to him and worked it out instead. So why suddenly drop the case?"

Anderson folded the paper and slid it into his suit pocket, probably in case we needed to pull it out to show to Leonard. "Fair enough."

The Albrights didn't live in Fair Haven like Gordon had. Instead, they were in another little town, closer to Grand Rapids.

The distance actually worked in our favor, assuming Leonard was guilty. He wouldn't have been able to get to Gordon's home in Fair Haven, kill him, plant the body, clean up, and drive all the way back home without some sort of a trail. Someone must have noticed his absence, though his wife and children probably wouldn't be willing to testify against him. Or his receipts might show a purchase along the way.

The Albrights lived in a middle class-looking cul-de-sac near the middle of town. Once I'd found the lawsuit, I'd continued to dig into Leonard. He was a licensed counselor and had a successful practice.

Which was a bad thing for us. He'd be trained in picking up on subtle cues in tone and body language. Anderson and I would both need to be careful not to give anything away.

We'd also dressed like we were going to court. The first impression would matter.

The woman who opened the door had sandy-blonde shoulder-length hair and a smattering of freckles across her nose. The fact that I could see them spoke volumes about her. Most women tried to cover up any seeming imperfection with makeup. It made me like her. She was comfortable in her own skin.

We introduced ourselves, and she took us into the kitchen. An interesting choice. The natural place to meet would have been the living room.

She motioned toward the table. "I'd normally invite you into the living room where it's more comfortable, but our daughter has friends over, and they're watching a movie."

A shiver ran over my neck and back. She couldn't have known

what I was thinking, so we were either a bit alike in our thinking or she was also good at reading people. I hoped it wasn't the latter. It was bad enough that her husband's profession gave him an advantage.

As she was setting mugs of coffee in front of us, the kitchen door swung open. The man who entered looked nothing like Gordon Alright, and for a second, I thought I'd called the wrong Leonard Albright. Where Gordon had dressed the part for someone working at a chainsaw and logging museum in his jeans and plaids— at least from all the pictures I'd seen—Leonard had the trendy look of someone who spent too much time keeping up on the latest fashions for a man. Or for a woman, for that matter.

He offered me his hand. It was softer than mine. "I'm glad you felt comfortable calling us. It was a shock when the police told us they'd arrested Clement. He and Gordon have been friends for years, and Gordon worked for Clement's father before that. I'd much rather it turned out someone else was behind this."

His tone was too smooth for my taste. It gave me the same feeling as drinking a medicine that left a slick coating on my throat.

Mrs. Albright laid a plate of store-bought chocolate chip cookies in the center of the table and nudged it toward us. "We talked about it after you called, though, and we couldn't come up with anyone who might have wanted to hurt Gordon. He was liked by everyone who knew him."

Crap. I'd worried that with such a long break between when I called and when we'd been able to meet it would give them too much time to come up with their story if they had something to hide. Though perhaps the fact that she'd admitted to them talking about it indicated innocence. I wasn't getting a clear enough read on either of them to tell. They both seemed unnaturally calm.

That alone made me think they had something to hide. Talking to lawyers in a criminal case made normal people nervous.

And if they wanted to get away with something, claiming they didn't know of anyone else who would have wanted to hurt Gordon would be a smart move. The police were convinced Clement did it. Why muddy the waters and risk them taking a closer look?

I could feel Anderson waiting for me. This was my case. I needed to lead.

But I needed to be careful about how I broached the lawsuit since I didn't want my suspicions to be obvious, and I didn't want them to kick us out.

I placed a cookie on the napkin in front of me as a way to add a casualness to my next words. "It's hard sometimes to think of who might want to hurt a loved one because we never would. But we found something."

I held out my hand toward Anderson. He pulled the paper from his pocket and laid it out on the table in front of them, close enough that they could read it.

I touched the nearest edge with my fingertips. "If he stole money from your mother, it's possible he also stole money from other people."

Leonard continued to stare down at the paper as if he were reading it carefully. The long hair at the front of his haircut drooped onto his forehead, and he brushed it back. I'd never been a fan of that style. It always reminded me of a man using a comb-over to hide his balding spot.

Leonard met my gaze, and his expression didn't even flicker. He was too well-trained. He'd spent too many years hearing shocking things from clients while having to maintain a straight face. Nothing I could say was going to rattle him. The best I could hope for would be to find an inconsistency somewhere and push at it.

"Gordon wouldn't have stolen money from anyone," Leonard said.

It was an interesting way of phrasing it. The lawsuit said he believed his brother embezzled from their mother, but he hadn't said *anyone else*. He'd said *anyone*, which technically included their mother. I couldn't reconcile the two, but I knew he was hiding something the same way I knew from a seemingly innocent tickle in the back of my throat that I was coming down with a cold.

I made sure to give him my best paragon-of-innocence look. "He stole from your mother."

The implication was clear enough that I let it hang. It was a technique used by counselors as well as lawyers, so I knew Leonard would recognize it for what it was. He'd also have to respond to it, though. If he didn't, it'd point a spotlight at that area of questioning just as much as when I avoided leading statements in my therapy sessions.

"Gordon took money from our mother, but not because he's a thief."

Everything this man said was so carefully phrased it made me want to scream.

Mrs. Albright crossed her arms on the table in front of her, creating a bit of a blockade between us. Interesting. Maybe I was aiming my questions at the wrong person. She'd learned from years spent married to a counselor, but she likely didn't have the same professional training he did. I might be able to crack her if I couldn't crack him.

I shifted slightly so that my next statement could appear to be directed at either of them.

"He took something that didn't belong to him. That's what it means to be a thief."

I looked at her as I finished.

Her chair creaked slightly underneath her, as if she'd wrapped her feet around the legs. "I don't understand why Gordon's on trial here. Nothing he did should matter now."

This had to be one of the most confusing interviews I'd ever done. Now I couldn't be sure whether they were trying to hide something that would implicate them in Gordon's death or whether they were trying to hide Gordon's sins. Many people did think that, when a person died, all their flaws and failings should be erased from memory.

As a criminal lawyer, that was the opposite of what I needed to do. The roots for motive came both from the guilty party and from what the victim might have done while alive.

The tricky part of that when speaking to the victim's family was that you couldn't make it seem like you were blaming the victim at all. Not only would it make them defensive, but it would compound their grief.

"Gordon's not on trial. In fact, the Dodds had nothing but praise for him. Which is what makes this so confusing. If the police are right, we have to believe that Clement Dodd killed his best friend for no reason. I want to be sure that there wasn't some other reason Gordon was killed."

I made sure to avoid saying *someone else who might have killed him*.

Her head twitched in the direction of Leonard as if she wanted to look at him but caught herself. "Gordon was a good man."

Another sidestep. We might as well be dancing.

I slid the paper on the table closer to her. "You two felt wronged enough about the situation with your mother-in-law to bring this suit against him. It speaks to Gordon perhaps being involved in other things as well. That doesn't mean he wasn't a good man. It doesn't mean he deserved to die. All we're trying to do is figure out *why* he died."

Leonard planted a hand on the paper and drew it back toward him. "I brought this suit over a misunderstanding. Nothing more. It had nothing to do with Gordon's death."

His soft spot is his wife, the little voice in my head whispered.

I filed the knowledge away for future reference. "If you could explain it to me, that would really help. Right now, I'm wondering if Gordon stole from the museum and Clement found out."

Anderson sat like a rock beside me, quietly dunking a cookie in his coffee and acting as if I hadn't just pulled that out of thin air.

"Why did you drop the suit against your brother, Mr. Albright?" I infused enough of a lawyer's tone into my voice that I hoped he'd feel compelled to give me a clear answer this time.

He folded his hands over top of the paper. "I found out why he took the money."

It was the first non-equivocal statement he'd made since we walked in.

"And why did he take the money?" Anderson asked.

I held back a smile. That couldn't have been more perfectly played if we'd planned it. Had I asked the question, it could have started to feel too much like an attack. With Anderson switching it up, it should feel more like a conversation.

"Drugs," Leonard said.

The table rocked, and Mrs. Albright cringed as if she'd hit her knee on the underside.

Leonard took a cookie from the plate in the center of the table as if nothing had happened. If banging her knee hadn't been a reaction to what he just said, I would have expected him to ask if she were okay. By pretending like nothing had happened, he gave himself away.

Something about his story upset his wife.

"Gordon confessed what happened to me." Leonard sat the cookie in front of himself without actually eating it. "He begged my forgiveness, and I gave it and dropped the suit. At that point, my concern was finding him help, but he told me he'd already been clean for a while and had a sponsor. He was even willing to make amends if that's what it took."

Mrs. Albright hadn't reacted again, but she was staring at her cup. She'd been almost as hard to read as Leonard until now. That could mean a lot of things, but my instincts said it was because Leonard was lying to me. He'd also gone off whatever script they'd come up with together.

"Could you give me the name of Gordon's sponsor? I want to

make sure he really was clean. If he slipped, he might not have had the money to pay his dealer, and that could have gotten him killed."

The holes in that story were big enough that Velma could have slept in them. A dealer wouldn't have bothered dragging Gordon's body into Clement's home to frame him for the crime. A dealer would have shot Gordon and let him lie where he fell.

"The A in NA stands for anonymous." Leonard rose to his feet. "Even though Gordon's no longer with us, his sponsor's privacy should be respected. I'm sorry, but I don't think there's anything else we can tell you that would help. We wish Clement hadn't done this, but it looks like he did. Not everything in life makes sense."

Leonard saw us to the door.

I climbed back into the car, but didn't let my posture or expression change until we were down the street and I was sure Leonard Albright couldn't see me anymore.

I pulled a face. "I'm certain they're lying about something."

"I'd hate for the prosecution to call him as a witness in any of my cases. He was unshakeable until you went for his wife. But that doesn't necessarily mean they were lying. It's possible they just didn't want to tell you about Gordon's past drug history. If they think Clement did it, they had to know you would argue what you did and try to present that as reasonable doubt for getting Clement acquitted."

I wanted to argue, but he was right. It was possible Mrs. Albright had reacted because she and her husband had decided they weren't going to tell anyone about Gordon's drug history. It was also possible she'd reacted because she hadn't known about his drug problem.

If that was the case, one thing still bothered me about it all. Neither Clement nor Darlene had mentioned that Gordon had a drug problem when I asked them about people who might have wanted to hurt Gordon. There was no way they wouldn't have noticed a drug problem in someone they spent so much time with. They'd either hid it from me, or something else was going on here—potentially something that led to Gordon Albright's death.

10

J dropped Anderson off at his car, but before I could decide whether to head home or try to make it to where Clement was being held before they closed to visitors, my phone dinged with a text notification.

I'm worried about Russ, Stacey wrote. *He had chest pains today.*

Stacey's text validated my concerns for Russ. I'd been afraid I'd been overreacting. Though knowing I'd been right wasn't much of a comfort. It seemed like Russ had stopped caring about his health after Noah and my Uncle Stan died. But he didn't want to talk about it or acknowledge it in any way.

The fact that Stacey texted me meant she expected me to have some solution. And I didn't.

When my Uncle Stan had his drinking problem, my dad's solution had been to pretend like it didn't exist. At the time, I'd thought it was because he didn't want to tarnish the family image by admitting his brother was an alcoholic. Understanding my dad a little better now, though, it could also have been because he didn't know what to do about it, and the one thing my dad hated more than anything was to feel helpless or inept.

All of us pretending Uncle Stan didn't have a problem resulted in him developing a dangerous heart condition. I refused to do the same with Russ.

I backed out of the parking lot and headed to Fair Haven. I'd wait to talk to Clement until tomorrow. I wouldn't be able to concentrate on his case properly right now anyway.

Forget concentrating, I wouldn't be able to sleep until I had some sort of plan for how to help Russ.

My parents believed a lot of things that I didn't, but one area where we agreed was that if you needed information on something or you needed something done and you weren't an expert in that area, you should find the best person in that field and ask or hire them.

The best specialist when it came to health would be Russ' doctor, but he wouldn't discuss a patient's health with someone else without the patient's express permission. Even though I technically had power of attorney for health for Russ, that legally only took effect if he couldn't make decisions for himself anymore.

But Saul might be willing to give me some advice as long as I kept the conversation general. He dealt with people's health concerns on a daily basis, and he'd probably seen more than I could imagine. He also knew I had permission to pick up Russ' medications, so it wasn't like I was being nosy for the thrill of it.

Once I hit the main street, I took the next turn rather than heading straight through the traffic light to continue on to Sugarwood.

The pharmacy was busy when I entered, so I wandered the aisles for fifteen minutes until all the other customers had picked up their prescriptions and left.

The whoosh-whoosh of wheels turning behind me told me Saul had decided to seek me out rather than wait for me to return to the counter. This was the first time I'd ever browsed the aisles rather than coming in and heading straight for something specific.

I turned around.

Saul sat in his chair a couple of feet behind me. "I don't remember filling anything for you, Nicole, and I know Russ' medications aren't due for a refill. Did you need help finding something on the shelves?"

I returned the vitamin bottle that I'd been reading the label of for the third time to the shelf. "Sort of. I have a health concern that I was hoping you'd be able to give me some advice on."

Saul rolled himself backward manually. "Why don't we head to the counter?"

It felt like something had lodged in my throat where my neck met my torso. I wouldn't have had any problem coming to Saul for a recommendation on cold tablets or even something grosser, like athlete's foot. This was different. It felt more personal in a strange way.

I hopped up onto the seat next to his consultation counter. When I'd first met Saul and he'd still been walking, he used to sit on a stool on the other side. His chair was too low for that now. Instead, he maneuvered his chair next to me.

His back tire caught on a display rack of discounted sunscreen. It lurched to one side.

I leapt for it, but it toppled over, spewing sunscreen all over the floor.

I dropped to my knees and collected them.

Saul cursed. "The aisles aren't wide enough to be wheelchair-accessible. This happened last week, too, and I had to call in Victor to clean it up."

It would have been humiliating for him to have to call his boss over that. Nothing in this place was accessible for people with disabilities. Not really. It'd been built so long ago and never upgraded. "That's something else you can change when it's yours. I've seen some people with those wheeled walkers struggling, too."

Saul's fingers stretched out, then contracted. "Unfortunately, that's not going to happen."

I stopped re-stacking the tubes on the shelf so I could swivel for a better look at his face. His lips were tight, like he was clenching his teeth. Had he looked into it already, and renovating the pharmacy after he bought it was too expensive? His medical bills from his surgery had likely been massive. Maybe they'd eaten through his savings. "I'm sure if it's a cost thing we could put out a call for help in the community. There are a lot of people with construction or mechanical skills who I'm sure would be willing to help."

Saul must have realized he was clenching his body so tight he looked like he was ready to shatter. He visibly shook it off. His hands flattened on the arms of his chair. "Victor sold this place to someone else. He gave me the news yesterday."

Oh no. For as long as I'd been coming here, Saul had been

talking about the changes he wanted to make when this place was his. It was what originally got us past the professional pharmacist-patient level because I'd worn myself down with managing the changes I'd been making at Sugarwood and came in asking about vitamins and immune boosters.

I set down the tubes I was holding and dropped to my bottom on the floor. "I'm really sorry. He didn't warn you or anything?"

He shook his head. "He said he knew I couldn't match the offer the new owner made him. The new owner is a pharmacist as well, so I'll be lucky to even keep my hours."

The tone in his voice reminded me of how I'd felt the first time I screwed up in court and almost destroyed our client's whole case. It'd been the moment when I began to wonder if I'd made a mistake that I'd regret my whole life. I'd spent years in school and clerking.

If he'd been planning the rest of his career and his retirement based on the belief that he'd be able to buy this store, Saul could feel like he'd thrown away his future the way I'd felt I sabotaged mine. It was exactly what I didn't want to happen to me ten or twenty years down the road. I didn't want to make the wrong choice now and look back later to see I'd made a huge mistake.

Had I known him better, I would have hugged him. As it was, I didn't know what to do or what to say. I didn't have the ability to fix it—which seemed like a pattern for me lately—and everything that came to my mind to say sounded trite.

I settled on "I'm sorry." It might have been a cliché, but it was true.

His shoulders bounced slightly, like an exhausted man's version of a shrug. "You had a question for me, didn't you?"

I'd almost forgotten why I'd come in the first place. I scooped up another cluster of sunscreen tubes and arranged them on the next shelves, trying to match them to the price labels since I wouldn't actually be helping Saul if he had to come back and fix what I'd done later. It felt like the least I could do to make his day the tiniest bit better.

Now that I knew he had a new boss, I also wanted to be extra careful how I phrased my questions. I didn't want him getting in trouble on my behalf for violating confidentiality. His old boss gave him a lot of freedom. The new owner might keep a tighter watch.

"I need some advice. There's someone who is very important to me, and I'm worried about their health."

His expression was patient, and he wasn't fidgeting, but I could see the tiny shift in his gaze that said *Why are you talking to me about this?*

"Anyway, since you're Fair Haven's only pharmacist, I figured you'd seen people with a lot of different conditions and you might have some tips for me on how to talk to my friend."

"You want me to help you figure out how to get your friend to take your concerns seriously?"

Taken on its own, his reply could have implied I was being ridiculous, but his tone said he was merely trying to make sure he'd understood me correctly. I nodded.

He ran his hands back and forth along the top of his wheels in the same way someone else might pace while thinking. "I don't know that I can advise you as a pharmacist, but maybe I can as someone who lost a person they cared about to a health condition."

I finished replacing the sunscreen and sat cross-legged in front of him. I felt a bit like a student with a mentor. "I'm grateful for whatever guidance you can give me."

"My only sister had anorexia. I tried to talk to her, but her husband liked his women skinny, and she was willing to do anything to keep him from leaving her for someone thinner or younger or prettier."

I bit down on my bottom lip. He'd used the past tense. It could be that he meant it in the sense of *my sister once had anorexia and now she doesn't*, but the undertone of anger in his voice told me that wasn't where this was headed.

"It eventually killed her. Her heart couldn't take the strain anymore and gave out."

His voice was calm, but he rubbed his thumbs along the tips of his fingers, leaking the emotions that I was sure were rolling around inside. I had a theory that you never really got over the death of someone you loved. You re-learned how to live your life in a world where they didn't exist, and you found joy again, but you never stopped missing them.

Even a year later, I still had a lot of moments where I wanted to ask my Uncle Stan's advice on something, or talk about the latest mystery novel I'd read to see if I'd guessed the murderer before him, or just hear his laugh because I couldn't remember what it sounded like anymore.

I couldn't lose Russ too soon as well. I just couldn't. Not if there was anything I could do to prevent it.

Saul flattened his palms on his knees. "So I can't give you advice as a professional, but I can tell you what I wished I'd done. If I could do it over again, I wouldn't have tried to talk to her alone. I'd have collected a group of people who loved her. And I would have tried to convince her to go to counseling."

I crawled to my feet and brushed off my knees and bottom. Then I held out my hand to Saul. Granted, you didn't normally shake hands with your pharmacist, but this was a bit different. "Thank you."

Saul took my hand. "I won't say it was my pleasure, but I hope it helps."

As soon as I was back in my car, I called Mark and told him about Stacey's text and what Saul recommended.

"You're really starting to be a local, you know," Mark said. "You know almost more people than I do in the town at this point."

I highly doubted that since Mark was not only the county medical examiner, but also a Cavanaugh, and his family ran the local funeral home. But I took it as a compliment anyway. "Do you think an intervention might work? You, Stacey, and I aren't the only people who care about him and are worried."

In the silence, I could hear him moving papers around, so he must be in his office. I'd gotten good at knowing where he was based on the noises in the background and whether he answered his phone immediately or not. If I had to leave a message, he was either at a crime scene or in the middle of an autopsy. Mark was very careful about being professional about his cell phone use.

"Russ is extremely private," he finally said.

Russ was someone who eschewed the small-town gossip mill.

He didn't like to discuss any local news, and he was extra-careful not to say anything about anyone that could make its rounds of the town and come back warped. He certainly hadn't reacted well the few times I'd tried to pry into areas he felt I didn't belong.

But I was out of other ideas if Mark shot this one down. "I'm worried about him."

"I know. I am, too. We just can't rush in. Why don't you set up a time for you and me and Stacey to meet and talk about it? If we approach it wrong, or invite too many people, it'll backfire on us. If we embarrass him rather than making him feel loved, he'll take worse care of himself, not better."

11

When the guard ushered me into the private visiting room reserved for inmates meeting with their lawyers, Clement was already waiting for me.

Based on the visits I'd had with him in the Fair Haven police station, I'd expected to be brought down to his cell and have to talk to him through the bars while all his neighbors listened. Though perhaps that wasn't allowed here or Clement hadn't wanted anyone to overhear us or both. I wasn't complaining. Going into the actual cell block wouldn't have been a safe or smart idea.

Clement looked a little better than the last time I'd seen him. His skin wasn't as translucent, and the dark circles under his eyes were more smudges than purple paint smears now. It's amazing what a little hope would do for a person. Knowing I had a lead on another possibility for what happened to Gordon should bring his spirits up even more.

The guard let me know he'd be outside the door and showed me how to contact him when I was ready to leave.

The door closed with a clang, and Clement and I were alone. My mind tried to freeze. Because if he decided to hurt me, my odds of notifying the guard in time weren't good.

I gave myself a mental shake. That was the PTSD talking. I could recognize it now. Recognizing it didn't stop the jittery feeling in my body like a nest of spiders was trying to crawl out of my stomach, but it meant I could keep it from controlling me.

We haven't proven Clement is a killer, I reminded myself. *You don't need to be afraid of a potentially innocent man.*

The little fear devil that liked to sit on my metaphorical shoulder and whisper in my ear tried to remind me that, if Clement was guilty, he was the kind of person who couldn't control his actions, and no one was safe with him.

One of the things I'd been talking about with my counselor was techniques I could use to make myself feel safer. Planning an escape route was one of them. I'd found it especially helpful in situations where I didn't have the time to repeat Bible verses to myself.

I edged my chair back so that I could evacuate it quickly and use it as a barricade to buy myself time, just in case. "I spoke with Leonard Albright and his wife. They told me a few things about Gordon that could point to other people who might have had a motive for hurting him."

I left out the question floating on the back of my tongue about why he and Darlene hadn't mentioned it. It would have sounded accusatory no matter how I phrased it. My dad had drilled it into me that you had to keep your client feeling like you were their ally. The worst thing you could do was to make them feel like you were attacking them as well.

"They weren't as forthcoming with details as I needed, though," I said, "so I was hoping you could fill in the gaps."

Clement scratched at the bottom of his beard with his knuckles. "He and Gordon haven't spoken since right after their mother passed. I'm surprised Leonard had anything useful to tell you."

The way everyone kept saying that, it made me think they'd been close before. Not all families were. Some people only saw their relatives at weddings and funerals and felt that was too much. "Leonard told me about Gordon's drug addiction."

Clement's eyebrows went up, but stayed in two straight lines instead of forming V's the way Mark's did. He tugged on his ear. "He told you Gordon had a drug addiction."

I couldn't tell if it was a statement or a question. Which meant I also couldn't tell if Clement was surprised they'd told me or was surprised because of what they'd told me. "That's what they said."

He kept tugging on his ear—enough that I was almost afraid he was going to permanently stretch it out.

He didn't have to say it now. I knew from Clement's body language. Leonard Albright lied to me. Gordon hadn't had a drug addiction. Still, because of what was at stake, I had to hear him confirm it. "Gordon didn't have a drug problem, did he?"

Clement shook his head.

"Leonard said Gordon stole their mom's money to fund his drug habit, and that's why there was nothing left of her estate. Leonard dropped the suit when he found out because Gordon was getting help."

Clement drew in one of those breaths that said someone was stalling for time. It let me know that his pause wasn't due to another one of his lapses in concentration. "I don't understand."

"You're sure Gordon didn't struggle with drugs? Addicts can be good at hiding it."

"I've known addicts before, Ms. Dawes. Physical symptoms, they show eventually. Darlene and I spent twelve hours or more a day with Gordon. Even if I thought my best friend would hide that from me, I don't think he could. Not if his habit was progressed enough to consume his mother's entire estate prior to her death."

That was a reasonable argument. "Then I won't waste time looking for his drug dealer. What did Gordon tell you happened with the lawsuit?"

"That's why I don't understand it. Gordon and Leonard's mother was so sick near the end of her life that Gordon looked into natural pain remedies to supplement the morphine. From what Gordon told me, her care ate up all her assets."

Why would Leonard lie to me if that was the case? Had he refused to believe the truth, and so Gordon fed him a lie that would be more acceptable to a counselor?

The only other alternative seemed to be that Gordon had managed to deceive those closest to him about a major drug habit. I tended to agree with Clement that, given how much time they spent together, even a functional drug addict wouldn't have been able to disguise all the signs. Even Leonard claimed not to have known about it prior to their mother's death, and yet they'd been close enough that their relational break drew attention. And I had to believe that Gordon's mother wouldn't have given him complete control over her finances if she'd suspected anything of the sort.

But if Gordon wasn't a drug addict, then it left me with one key question I had to answer above anything else related to this case— why had Leonard Albright lied?

12

*B*efore I left, I reminded Clement that I'd set up a psychological and medical forensic evaluation for him. If I figured out that someone else killed Gordon, and had evidence for who that someone was, we wouldn't need the evaluation results, but I didn't want to take chances.

I might not be able to prove that someone else had done it with enough certainty to get the case dismissed. I might be able to prove it with enough certainty for Clement and Darlene, though, and in that case, we'd want to fight to the end to minimize Clement's sentence even if I couldn't get him acquitted. An evaluation that confirmed his diagnosis and that confusion and hallucinations were possible would help.

Once I was back at my car, I called Chief McTavish and arranged to be let in to Gordon's house. Since the prosecution went through his home, I was allowed the opportunity as defense counsel as well. The police and prosecutor would have been looking for anything that could implicate Clement. I had to see if I could figure out the truth behind what happened to Gordon's mother's money.

Before heading to Gordon's house, I went by the Fair Haven post office and mailed the letter Clement gave me. It was the first non-business correspondence I'd ever had to mail. With email and texting, I didn't realize people actually even wrote letters anymore.

Clement was trying to put his affairs in order the way his doctor had suggested, though, and he'd wanted to write a letter thanking the teacher who'd gotten him interested in history. Given the man's age, Clement suspected he didn't have email, and it wasn't like Clement was allowed a lot of phone time in prison.

Clement hadn't had an address, so I'd had to get the clerk's help figuring it out. She'd even called over one of Fair Haven's mailmen. The mailman knew my name because he also delivered to Sugarwood, and I'd left him a bottle of maple syrup in the mailbox at Christmas. The clerk went to my church.

A warm little shiver filled my core. Mark had been right. I was a local now. I belonged. That revelation made me even gladder we'd decided to stay in Fair Haven.

By the time we finished dealing with that single letter, I was running late. Chief McTavish had said he was sending someone to meet me at Gordon's house right away, and I didn't want to waste that officer's time by keeping him or her waiting.

Troy Summoner already stood next to his police cruiser in Gordon Albright's driveway when I pulled up.

He touched the brim of his hat. "The chief said I need to go in with you."

I hadn't expected to be allowed to go in alone—they couldn't risk a shady defense attorney planting evidence and claiming to have found it. Someone had to corroborate whatever I saw here. Even though I wasn't dishonest, policy was policy.

I smiled at him. "Don't worry. I won't leave a mess."

He gave me the staid blink-blink that I took as appreciation of my teasing. He was much too young to be this serious. I'd appreciated it when I was the victim, though. Troy helped the day my dogs were kidnapped, and he took the situation seriously, unlike the first officer who responded—Grady Scherwin. Scherwin was the Fair Haven officer I liked the least.

Troy unlocked the special padlock that was on the door.

Gordon's house still carried a hint of antiseptic. It hit my nose sharply, and I could almost taste it on the back of my tongue. Not a smell I usually associated with a personal dwelling. It was more heavy-duty-hospital-disinfectant smell.

Troy stayed quiet and trailed behind me as I went from room to room. The bathroom still had a raised seat and handrails alongside the toilet, and the tub had been cut away on the side and a door installed so that a person wouldn't have to step over the side to get in.

I peeked into the nearest bedroom down the hall. A hospital-style bed that could be raised and lowered electronically and had rails along the side rested where the bed normally would, and a wheelchair lurked in the corner. I wasn't a medical expert, but the canister attached to the chair looked like oxygen.

According to Maryanne Albright's obituary, she'd died almost a year ago, not long after my Uncle Stan. That was a long time to keep expensive medical equipment around without reselling it, especially if someone had the level of drug problem Leonard claimed Gordon had. Even if he'd gotten clean shortly after, he likely would have sold the equipment to repay his brother for some of what he'd taken if he was penitent.

I'd been in the house of an addict before. To fund and then pay off his debts from his gambling addiction, Noah had stripped his house bare. Gordon still had a fairly large TV in the living room alongside the medical equipment.

If Leonard's story sprung any more holes, I could use it as a sieve.

Knowing that didn't help me, though, unless I could figure out what was really going on between the brothers.

"Is there anything specific you're looking for?" Troy asked from behind me. "We took the computer out of the house to process if that's what you want."

"I'll ask Chief McTavish for the results."

I stopped in the doorway of the bedroom and tapped my finger on the frame. Whatever they found on the computer could be useful, but most people kept tax records in paper form. If Gordon had spent his mother's money on her medical care, he should have tax receipts. Hopefully he knew he was supposed to keep his tax records for seven years post-filing.

"Which room did they take the computer out of?"

I moved away from the doorway and Troy took me to the end of the hallway. Gordon's hallways were wider than most. If I stuck my arms out to either side of me, my fingers wouldn't have touched the sides. It was the perfect house for a person who needed a wheelchair.

Maybe that was why Maryanne Albright stayed with Gordon rather than with Leonard and his wife, where she would have had two people to care for her. Either that, or Gordon bought this house recently with his mother's needs in mind.

I should mention the house to Saul in case his current home wasn't as well suited.

Troy opened a door at the end of the hallway and stepped in. "It's a small room. Is there something you want me to bring out for you?"

A tight feeling filled my chest like a balloon inflating in a space two sizes too small. Troy was probably only trying to be helpful, but his presence was starting to feel a bit intrusive, and I couldn't shake the feeling that he either wanted to be done here or he was trying to block my investigation.

Neither made any sense. Chief McTavish wouldn't allow him to be part of this case if he had any connection with the victim or the accused. The more likely explanation was that Troy's personality and mine didn't mesh well. His desire to be fastidious and watch over everything was likely unintentionally pressing the button inside of me that reacted when I felt my abilities were being questioned.

And that was okay. I didn't need to have a friendship with every member of the Fair Haven police department. It was probably better that I didn't.

What I did need to do was find a way to work with him.

Which meant phrasing things carefully. I didn't want to make it sound like I didn't trust him to find what I wanted. We wouldn't work together any better if he thought I felt he wasn't smart enough to notice things.

"I need to take a look myself. My client wouldn't appreciate it if I wasn't personally managing looking into this aspect of his case."

He gave a grudging nod. We swapped places, but Troy stayed in the doorway. He still had the demeanor of a babysitter watching over a stubborn child, but at least he wasn't in my way anymore.

He hadn't been exaggerating when he said the space was a tight fit. The room wasn't much more than a closet. The desk where the computer must have sat was wedged up against one wall, and two filing cabinets stood along the perpendicular wall.

With only two filing cabinets, it wouldn't take me long to find what I was looking for. I pulled open the first drawer. It was empty.

I looked back over my shoulder at Troy. "Did the police take any paperwork?"

Troy shook his head. "Computer only. They looked through the cabinets, but I guess nothing there was pertinent."

They didn't know to look for evidence that Gordon had stolen from his mother because they were only looking for evidence that Clement killed him. Even if they'd seen financial paperwork, they wouldn't think to examine it. So their idea of *pertinent* and mine would be different.

The next drawer contained nothing but blank printer paper, still in its packaging. There wasn't a printer on the desk. Would there be a reason for someone to take his printer? Maybe I simply hadn't noticed it. Space was limited. I craned my neck and looked under the desk. There was the printer. Minor mystery solved.

The second filing cabinet contained all the warranty information and manuals for the medical equipment and appliances. The fourth drawer was empty again.

I wanted to slump down, but Troy was still watching. Unless I could find something to refute Leonard's story, I'd never get the truth. He had no reason to tell me anything other than what he had. I didn't know what the truth might be, so I didn't know where to look beyond here.

"I shouldn't be away from the station too long," Troy said.

Patience, Nikki. Patience.

And he can learn some patience too, the imp in the back of my mind said.

Police work wasn't all about the excitement of watching over suspects. He might feel like he was missing out on something more interesting here, but this was part of police work, too.

I smiled serenely at him. "Investigations can be a bit tedious at times. I shouldn't be too much longer, but I have to make sure I don't miss something important that could hurt the case."

Nothing changed in his expression. The thought that he probably wouldn't even sneeze if I tickled his nose with a feather flitted across my mind.

But he was going to get his wish. I was done here unless I could figure out where else Gordon might have stored paperwork if not in his office. He'd have had no reason to hide it in his own house.

When I was sorting through Uncle Stan's belongings after he passed away, I'd found some boxes of old records up in the attic. "Does this house have an attic?"

"Nope."

Strike that one. A garage might function the same way, though.

I headed back down the hall to the door off the kitchen that connected to the small one-car garage.

Mail rested on Gordon's kitchen table—likely from the day he died or the day before—already opened. I flipped through them, making sure not to make eye contact with Troy in case he disapproved. Two of them were bills, and both showed that he wasn't carrying an overdue balance.

If he was a drug addict, he was the most responsible, conscientious one I'd ever seen.

The ramp into the house for Maryanne Albright's wheelchair ran up to the front door, suggesting that Gordon brought her in that way. It was possible he used the garage for storage rather than for parking his car.

I pushed open the door. The car wasn't parked inside, but he did have a push lawnmower. And shelves filled with clear plastic tubs. I walked along beside them and peered into each. Winter clothes. Tools.

Papers.

Jackpot.

Since the bin was at head height, I pointed at it. "I need that one, please."

Troy didn't audibly sigh, but I could have sworn I felt a disturbance in the Force, as a *Star Wars*' character might say. He got it down for me anyway. He must have realized that, the quicker he complied, the sooner we'd get out of here.

I couldn't imagine that the cement floor would be warm, and there wasn't anything useful to sit on nearby. I squatted down next to the bin and popped the lid.

It wasn't simply papers inside. These were definitely tax returns.

I pulled out the previous year for Gordon. Gordon's income was in line with what I'd seen of the house and his car. Yet another thing that didn't line up with him having a drug addiction. If it'd been ongoing for long, he should have already lost his house, or there should have been overdue notices. Addicts tended to rack up bills quickly, and paying them off even once they got clean took time.

I wriggled out the next bundle, and a bank book fell out. No one I knew stored their bank book in the garage or with their tax returns. This could belong to Maryanne Albright and Gordon put it with the tax returns when he was compiling evidence for his defense in the suit Leonard brought.

The tax return package bulged. A glance inside showed not only the return but a sheaf of what looked like receipts. This was going to take me longer than a few minutes to sort through. Troy was going to *love* me after this.

I straightened. "This is what I was looking for, but I can't examine it out here."

I hurried back into the house before he could ask any questions, moved the bills from the table, and laid out the tax return.

Troy stared down at the papers with what could almost be classified as a scowl. "How does this apply to Clement Dodd's case? I can't let you scrounge around in material that's unrelated."

I had to remind myself that I couldn't kick him in the shin. It'd be assault on an officer of the law. I'd already spent a night in a cell for something I didn't do. I had no desire to go back, no matter how frustrating I found Troy at this moment.

"It's related to a motive someone else might have had for murdering Gordon Albright, and that creates reasonable doubt for my client." He'd been trying to speed this along the whole time. Maybe that would play in my favor. "I'd be able to finish with it sooner if you're willing to help."

He pulled out a chair and sat next to me.

That seemed like the closest to an acceptance as I was going to get. I handed him the stack of receipts that had the label *Medical* paper-clipped to them. "I need you to hand me these in order."

I grabbed a paper and pen and brought out my cell phone. If Gordon put this bank book with the tax receipts, it was a good bet he'd thought it would help make his case. So if I could find that the numbers matched, I'd be able to prove Gordon hadn't been taking money from his mother for drugs.

For the next hour and a half, Troy and I worked the numbers—and, to my surprise, he didn't complain anymore.

He put the paperclip back on the stack of receipts after I finished with the last one. Partway in, he'd seemed to catch on to the theory I was working, because when we came to a couple of receipts that looked like they might be forged, he called the company and confirmed they were legitimate for me.

"There are still gaps," I said.

There were enough gaps that I hadn't proved or disproved anything yet. The medical expenses matched almost every withdrawal in the bank book, but not all.

My gaze strayed to the remaining papers in the file. And I almost felt bad. Troy had been quite obliging since we sat down, and now I was going to have to push that.

His gaze followed mine, and he pulled the papers over and separated them into stacks. "Where do you want me to start?"

We'd never be besties, but he was growing on me a little.

Gordon had labeled everything else with a date and a line in the bank book, showing when he'd removed the money. He couldn't have known his brother would question him after their mother's death, so this must have simply been how he handled being a conscientious power of attorney. Or maybe he'd simply been the kind of man who didn't like to take chances—yet another feature that wouldn't match with a drug addict.

When we finished all the stacks, only one withdrawal remained unaccounted for.

The large one that nearly drained the account the week before Maryanne Albright died.

ordon Albright hadn't been a drug addict, but he might still have been a thief.

If he'd had a drug addiction, he would have been skimming money all along. That large withdrawal at the end made it look more like he'd known his mother was reaching the end of her life and wanted to take what was left of her money before she died. Upon death, her accounts would have been frozen, and his power of attorney would have ended. Then the estate would have been split between him and his brother, giving him only half.

He might have fed Leonard the drug addiction story himself to convince his brother to drop the suit. That didn't explain the strange reaction from Leonard's wife, though.

What would explain her reaction was if Leonard made up the drug addiction story to cover up the fact that he knew his brother stole that money and killed him over it.

If that was the case, he shouldn't have sued Gordon at all, but perhaps that was a mistake he realized once it was too late. Bringing the suit at all would make him a suspect if Gordon died under suspicious circumstances. If he dropped the suit, waited, and then planted Gordon's body in Clement's house, he had a chance of getting away with it.

Did he want vengeance more than he wanted the money returned? If he'd continued with the suit and won—which he might have since Gordon had no record of where that large sum of money went—he would have gotten his inheritance. Killing his brother got him nothing monetarily.

This case made me feel a bit like I was trying to run a marathon with one shoe on. I had to keep moving forward, but everything felt awkward.

I took a picture of the bank book on my phone, wrote down the name of the accountant Gordon Albright used, and then Troy and I packaged everything else back up and replaced it where we'd found it. I couldn't remove them without permission, and they'd be safe here anyway.

There was only one way to unravel this conundrum. Anderson and I had to go back and confront Leonard Albright and his wife with the evidence I'd found proving Gordon didn't have a drug addiction after all.

When I left Gordon's house, I called Chief McTavish on my drive home and asked about Gordon's financial records. They hadn't been included in the discovery package I received from the prosecution. Chief McTavish confirmed for me that they did look at his bank records, but there wasn't anything that stood out. Since the prosecution wasn't planning to use any of the information, it hadn't been included in what I'd been given.

I gave him the date and amount I was looking for specifically. "Did he have anything on that date or in the weeks that followed?"

"He didn't have that size of a deposit before or after that date." His voice had a what-are-you-up-to-now tone to it.

I wasn't about to tell him. We weren't exactly in agreement on this case.

Depositing what he'd taken from his mother in one large chunk would have made it too obvious. Maybe he'd done it slowly over time. "Did his deposits increase at all after that date?"

"Nope. Like I said, nothing in his financials stood out or pointed at anything going on that could have resulted in his death."

I thanked him and disconnected.

That was annoying. What had Gordon done with the money, hidden it in his mattress? It made it more difficult to argue that he'd merely stolen it if he hadn't somehow deposited it in his accounts. It made it look like he'd taken it to use for something.

Leonard would argue drugs, but nothing else pointed to that, so I still had enough to make a solid case that Leonard lied to us about what was going on between him and Gordon.

I called Anderson for his availability to go back to talk to Leonard again. The list of days was short. He hadn't been exaggerating when he said he was busy right now.

By the time I finished with Anderson, I was home. I put the car in park, but left it running so I'd have heat while I called Leonard

Albright. I wanted to get it done before it got any later, and once I went inside, my dogs would be clamoring for my attention.

Leonard's number rang so many times I thought he might not pick up.

"Albright," he answered on the fifth ring.

"This is Nicole Fitzhenry-Dawes, Clement Dodd's attorney. I have a few more questions I need to ask you, and I was hoping we could set up a time to meet."

"I've told you everything there is to tell, Ms. Fitzhenry-Dawes." His voice sounded the same as I imagined it would if he were talking to a patient who'd tried to overstep the personal-professional boundary. "I don't want to waste either of our time with another meeting. If you truly feel I have something germane to add to Clement's defense, you can summon me to appear in court."

And then he hung up on me.

I mimed whacking my phone off the steering wheel. That was both rude and final. Calling him back wouldn't do any good.

But I didn't want to wait to question him in front of the judge at the preliminary hearing to determine probable cause. A judge wouldn't even allow me to call Leonard to the stand unless I had more proof than a hunch that Gordon Albright wasn't a drug addict and that Leonard dropped the lawsuit with the plan to kill him rather than forgive him.

The truth was, I didn't know enough about what was happening to feel confident calling Leonard to the stand. I could end up looking like a fool, and that would be extremely bad for Clement's case. Besides, I had to establish that there was a reason to call Leonard as a witness prior to the pre-trial motions that would take place after the preliminary hearing. If I didn't, his testimony wouldn't even be allowed at the actual trial. And waiting until the trial to show someone else had killed Gordon meant Clement might die an innocent man in prison waiting for his trial date due to his fatal insomnia.

Too much was at stake to wait and gamble. I had to find another way to get Leonard Albright to talk to me.

"$\mathcal{D}$id you learn your unconventional methods from your dad?" Anderson asked as we rode the elevator up to Leonard Albright's office. "Because I don't remember reading anything about him accosting possible witnesses at their place of business."

After Leonard refused to see me, I'd called his office and booked an appointment with him under a fake name. The only part of the ploy that made me uncomfortable was I'd had to tell his receptionist that I was feeling depressed and was afraid I might become suicidal if I didn't speak to someone soon. Otherwise, she'd said he didn't have an opening for a new client for weeks.

I hated lying about something like that. Depression and suicide were serious and real mental health issues that cost lives every year.

"I'm not accosting him. I'm not even going to cause a scene. But if I'm paying for an appointment slot with him, he can't say I'm wasting his time."

Anderson scowled.

I hadn't told him how I planned to meet with Leonard Albright in the car. That part I regretted too. "I'm sorry I didn't tell you sooner. I've gotten used to working on my own. It'll take me a little bit to get back to working with a partner."

He didn't turn to look at me, but a smile played on his lips. "Does that mean you're going to accept my offer?"

I deserved a mental self-smack for falsely raising his hopes. "Maybe we should wait to see how the preliminary hearing goes. If I really botch it, you might want to retract your offer."

Anderson shook his head. "I suppose I have to accept that. I'm the one who pushed you to try arguing a case before you made the final decision."

Yes, he had.

"You don't have to look so smug about it," he said, but there was laughter in his voice.

I wiped my expression blank, and the elevator door opened, letting us off into the reception area of Leonard Albright's office. Anderson took a seat while I checked in with the receptionist. The plan was that he'd stay in the reception area as my backup. I'd hoped the receptionist would be in the office, and I wouldn't be in a building alone with Leonard, but I'd made that assumption before and ended up talking to a criminal by myself. I wasn't taking that chance again. Those who didn't learn from history and all that. I'd learned.

My palms went a little moist waiting for Leonard to come out. All the ways this could go very wrong played in my mind.

The doorway to Leonard's office opened and he called the fake name I'd given. I stood up.

Leonard's gaze shifted toward me, and something flickered across his face too quickly for me to identify. All he said was, "Come on in."

The door clicked shut behind me, and Leonard's lips drooped down at the edges. It was the biggest emotional display I'd seen from him.

He kept a hand on the door. "This is harassment."

His body language oozed passive-aggressiveness. He didn't want me here, and yet he blocked the door, holding it shut with his hand so I couldn't escape. He couldn't realize it, or he would have controlled it.

Along with the fact that he'd invited me into his office at all, his body language told me he wasn't going to kick me out. He didn't want his receptionist wondering why I'd left before the session time was over. He was afraid of someone asking questions. He'd probably been bluffing and hoping I wouldn't call him to the stand in court because then he would have had to perjure himself if he wanted to stick to his story.

That knowledge gave me the upper hand.

"I thought you might want to talk without your wife around. I know she doesn't know the truth about Gordon." I pulled the picture I'd taken of Maryanne Albright's bank book up on my phone and turned the screen toward him. "But I do. I know he wasn't a drug addict skimming from your mother's money. Until this withdrawal, everything he took was for your mother's care."

Leonard moved back from the door and cracked his knuckles.

The popping sent a shiver down my spine, but the trained-lawyer part of my brain whispered that it was the most honest gesture he'd made over both times I'd spoken with him. It was the kind of bad habit that people in professional careers worked hard to break. But those habits reared up again during moments of extreme stress.

If he hadn't cracked his knuckles, I might have doubted my interpretation of the situation. Now I knew to be patient. He was already uncomfortable. Silence would increase that.

He sat in one of the armchairs in the middle of the room. I took the one across from him. And then we stared at each other for what felt like five minutes.

I knew it wasn't that long because I was sitting right in front of the clock above his head, but we were both trying to play the same game. Counselors used some of the same technique as lawyers and police officers to get their clients to open up and share more than they otherwise would. Leonard was trying to trip me up as well. We were at a stalemate.

I rested my hands on the arms of the chair, intentionally keeping my body language open and confident since I knew he could read mine as well as I could read his.

"I'm going to tell you the argument I'm considering making in court, and then you can decide if you'd rather we talked about this here instead. That bank withdrawal makes it look like you were right when you brought the suit against Gordon. He abused his power of attorney to take the last of your mother's money right before she died, leaving you with nothing. That's a strong motive for murder."

He continued to stare at me for the span of three blinks, long enough that I almost cracked and gave up.

On blink four, he leaned forward slightly. "I want to ask a hypothetical question of you first."

Not what I expected, but if it would get me the truth at last, I'd play along. "Okay. I'll answer if I'm able."

"If a person didn't learn about a crime until after the fact, could they still be considered an accessory?"

That opened up more questions for me than I'd had before. Was he worried about protecting himself or his wife? His wife was his soft spot. If he'd told her after our last visit that he'd killed Gordon and the drug accusation was a lie to hide it, then he might be worried the police would charge her with something as well.

"It depends on the situation. To be an accessory, a person"—I was careful not to say *you* in order to keep it general—"had to have helped with covering up the crime or had to help the perpetrator avoid capture. And spouses can't ever be forced to testify against their husband or wife."

"What about failure to report? As a therapist, I have a duty to report child abuse. Is there any law in place where an average citizen needs to report a crime that isn't child abuse if they learned about it months later and didn't participate in covering it up? All that person did was stay quiet once they learned of it."

He asked the questions so calmly that it raised the hairs on the back of my neck. If I hadn't known it was his training hiding his emotions, I would have pegged him for a sociopath. As it was, that knuckle crack made me think he was likely just really good at his job.

The second question also made it sound like it wasn't his wife he was worried about. Had Gordon committed some sort of crime and Leonard learned about it? If so, the victim of Gordon's crime could have come back later to exact revenge. Or someone else could have known about it and they were blackmailing Gordon. In that case, he would have taken the money to pay off his blackmailer.

I brought my hands down to my knees, a friendlier position. "You understand I can't give you legal counsel?"

He nodded, but the movement was abnormally small.

In many states, there wasn't even a legal duty to render aid to someone in distress. I'd had trouble sleeping for weeks after I heard about the Florida teens who videoed a man drowning on their phones and laughed rather than calling 911. Police were hoping to charge them with failure to report a death at least.

I doubted that's the kind of thing Leonard was talking about, though.

"As far as I know," I said, "there's no legal duty to report a crime in Michigan."

Leonard leaned forward slightly and put his hands on his knees as well, a mimic of my posture. "Gordon withdrew that money to purchase something for our mother that would help her peacefully end her own life."

15

That was not at all what I'd expected to hear.

I let myself slump back in the chair. Physician-assisted death was legal in only a handful of states, and only so long as they provided the means of death but didn't administer it.

Gordon wasn't a doctor, and Michigan wasn't one of the states where providing medical aid in dying was legal at all. If Gordon administered the lethal aid, then it would definitely have been considered a murder, even if he had been a doctor.

"Did your wife know?"

"She did. That's why she seemed shocked when I said Gordon had a drug addiction. I explained to her afterwards why I lied." Leonard's gaze shifted to the side and then back to me as if he was deciding how much to share with me. "Gordon refused to tell me at first where the money went. That's why I brought the suit against him. He only admitted it after that, and that's the real reason I dropped the lawsuit. Our mother was in so much pain those final weeks. If she asked Gordon to help end her suffering...it was a better use of her money than whatever I would have spent it on."

There was a fierceness to his voice that I hadn't heard before—a defense of his mother and brother's decision.

I'd never been there. I'd never had to watch someone I loved suffering. A part of me could understand their decision and a part of me couldn't. Life was a precious gift, and so many people who wanted more days didn't get to have them.

Despite that, it wasn't my place to criticize Leonard or Gordon right now. Right now, all that mattered was whether this somehow resulted in Gordon's death.

Whoever he bought the means of suicide from got their money. They wouldn't have had a reason to come after him or to frame Clement. It couldn't have been blackmail. That was the only unusual withdrawal from Maryanne Albright's account, and Gordon's financials hadn't shown anything unusual, according to Chief McTavish.

It was still possible that Leonard had killed Gordon because he was angry Gordon helped their mother end her life.

But I didn't see it. He sounded sincere when he'd defended Gordon's actions. He was good at hiding his emotions, but I hadn't seen any evidence that he was equally as good at faking emotions. Most people either had one of those skills or the other, but to have both was rarer.

"Why didn't you tell me about this when I first asked?"

"I thought my wife and I could be prosecuted after the fact for knowing about it, and I figured if I told you Gordon had a drug problem, you'd leave it at that or you'd pursue the drug angle and wouldn't find out the truth."

I almost had. If it hadn't been for Clement insisting Gordon didn't do drugs, I might have wasted a lot of time looking for a drug dealer who didn't exist.

With what was at stake, I had to make sure Leonard wasn't deceiving me again. If he hadn't planned to tell me that Gordon assisted their mother in killing herself, he might not have come up with a reason why I shouldn't think he'd want to punish Gordon for it. "Withholding information that way makes it seem like you might have been angry with Gordon for what he did and killed him over it."

"You could try that argument." Leonard crossed his legs. "But I was part of the committee that petitioned to have Michigan's laws concerning physician-assisted suicide changed. I'd be a hypocrite if I killed my brother because he wanted to provide the same peace to our mother that I wanted to provide to others."

His story was convincing except for one thing. "Then why weren't you two speaking again once you found out the truth?"

"I agreed with what he did, but he should have asked me rather than doing it on his own. I should have had my chance to say good-bye, too." Leonard's hands shifted toward each other like he wanted to crack his knuckles again. Instead his ran his fingers over his knuckles twice. "It seems stupid now that Gordon's gone, and my last words to him were angry ones. I didn't get to say goodbye to him, either." His hands separated, and he straightened his back. "Do you have any more questions, or are we done? The hour's almost up."

I didn't have any more questions. Not after that one sentence —*It seems stupid now.* Those were the words of someone who genuinely regretted not making up with a person they cared about before it was too late. He hadn't killed his brother.

Which meant I now had a much bigger problem.

It was back to looking like Clement was the only one who could have murdered Gordon Albright.

"IT'S POSSIBLE CLEMENT DID KILL GORDON," ANDERSON SAID ONCE we were back in my car.

It didn't help hearing my fear repeated back to me. Clement and I had a plan for what we'd do if we felt he was guilty. I just didn't want to execute it. I liked Clement, and I didn't want him to be guilty. I certainly didn't want him to have to spend his final days in prison, knowing his wife was afraid of him.

My phone vibrated in my pocket, and the Bluetooth display flashed the number for the prison where Clement was.

We had an appointment set up for visiting hours a couple of days after his psychological and medical assessments. There wasn't a reason he'd need to call me before then. The assessments weren't even scheduled until tomorrow.

Please God, let him not have been shanked in the shower and they're calling to tell me he's dead.

Or, worse, that he'd killed one of his fellow inmates. My chances of proving him innocent of Gordon's murder would be zero if he killed another person, regardless of the reasons.

I tapped the display screen. "This is Nicole. You're on speaker with co-counsel."

"I need to talk to you today." Clement's voice crackled in and out, like the landline he was on was too old to be reliable anymore.

I opened my mouth to ask if he could tell me whatever he needed to over the phone.

"In person," Clement said before I could. "In private."

I DROPPED ANDERSON BACK OFF AT HIS CAR AND HEADED ON. ON the drive, I called the prison and made sure they'd allow me to see Clement. I wasn't sure what the visiting hours were today, but I claimed I had to talk to him about an important element of his case that couldn't wait.

I could only assume that was the truth. I'd pushed for a bit more information, but Clement had refused to talk about it until I arrived.

The guard brought me back into the same room I'd met Clement in before.

Clement's skin was a healthy bronze tone, which was the opposite of what it should have been considering he'd been inside since his arrest except for the limited yard time prisoners received. His eyelids weren't drooping anymore, either, giving him a more alert look.

My body couldn't seem to get enough oxygen from the breaths I was taking. It was all wrong. He shouldn't have looked healthier than I'd ever seen him. Not even hope was that powerful.

I slid slowly into the chair across the table from him and waited, once again, for the guard to leave us alone. The door's clang as it shut seemed extra loud today. And my fear was for an entirely different reason.

The slightly out of breath feeling in my chest turned into an I've-been-running-up-a-steep-flight-of-stairs feeling. "You're looking much better," I said.

Clement rubbed a hand over his beard—slow like he was trying to coax out the words he needed to say. "I've been sleeping."

"How long?"

"Since I got here."

Oh crap, was the only words my mind could grapple on to. "I'm guessing your condition wasn't one that could spontaneously correct itself."

"Not according to my doctor. He told me to get my affairs in order."

Not just crap. Double crap. A whole truckload of crap-ness. If we couldn't prove Clement had fatal insomnia, then any defense based on him not understanding his actions was gone. We were claiming the insomnia caused hallucinations. If he didn't have fatal insomnia, he was lying about the hallucinations and sleep deprivation.

And there was a distinct possibility that I'd been played.

16

The cacophony of my own thoughts was so loud I wished my brain came with a mute button.

Clement shook his head. "I don't understa—"

I held up a finger. "I need you to sit quietly for a second. Please."

I examined his face. He met my gaze and didn't flinch away, even though it must have been uncomfortable to have me staring at him. The furrows in his forehead stayed identical to the way they'd been when I walked in, as if he'd been worrying about this long before I got there and was already concerned enough that my reaction wouldn't make it either better or worse.

Beyond all that, though, was the authenticity I'd thought I'd detected the first time we met, when I was talking to a man who loved his wife and his job and the history of Michigan. A man who was arrested because he was found over the body covered in blood, but who the police still hadn't been able to produce a motive for.

Had he tricked me?

It would have required extreme planning. He'd have had to know I was a lawyer before I told him because he'd shown signs of long-standing sleep deprivation from the moment I met him.

I ticked down one finger. If I got to three reasons in favor of his honesty, I'd give him the benefit of the doubt.

His timing was also terrible. If he'd been pretending, he should have kept pretending until after the psychological and medical assessments. There was no logical reason to pretend this long only to stop now. If he'd been faking, he'd been able to deceive trained professionals and should have been able to trick the ones I'd hired to assess him as well. I dropped another finger to the tabletop. That was two reasons.

Assuming he'd been telling me the truth about being diagnosed. "Will your doctor testify that you were diagnosed with fatal insomnia?"

"I can't see why not. It should also be in writing in my medical records, and he sent those to multiple specialists."

Okay, so then Clement would have had to be a talented actor, good enough to win an Oscar, to fool medical professionals. And he couldn't have faked the stress signs his body would have been showing. "I'll want you to sign a release so I can look at those records."

"Anything you need."

He didn't blink or hesitate. He was confident his records would show he'd indeed been suffering from fatal insomnia. That wouldn't be enough for the court if we couldn't prove he still was suffering now—the assumption would be that he'd tricked the original doctors but hadn't been able to trick the forensic specialists.

But it was enough for me.

I tapped my third finger into the desk, then tapped the three fingers together. Believing him left me in a real pickle, as my grandmother would have said.

"You said you started sleeping again after you came here."

"Within a night. I thought it was a fluke at first, so I didn't mention it, but it's been long enough now that I'm starting to feel like myself again."

If something as simple as a different bed would cure fatal insomnia, doctors would have figured it out long ago. Presumably the first thing they suggested to people who were struggling to sleep was to avoid caffeine, keep their room dark at night, and get a better mattress. The prison would have been noisier than his home, and the mattresses probably weren't nearly as comfortable as whatever Clement had at home. He should have slept worse, not better.

An underlying undiagnosed medical condition like restless leg syndrome or hyperthyroidism also wouldn't have cleared up simply because he ended up in prison, either.

The doctors said it wouldn't spontaneously correct itself, though, so *something* must have caused the change.

I rubbed at my temples. Maybe it would work some ideas to the surface. "Can you think of anything that's changed other than your surroundings?"

"The food's better at home."

I couldn't hold back a snort-laugh. Hospital food and airline food were usually the butt of jokes, but I had to think that was only because most people had never eaten prison food. It'd be ironic if the prison food healed him instead. But the only way that was possible was if he had an allergy.

Problem was, I didn't know if allergies could cause insomnia. I texted the question to Mark.

It'd be rare, he answered almost immediately. *But possible. Gluten most common.*

If it was an allergy, it'd be an undiagnosed one. "Is it the flavor that's better at home, or are you eating different types of foods here?"

Clement had his hand on his beard again. "The flavor. Everything here tastes like it came pre-packaged or they cooked it in a vat."

Snorting wasn't professional, so I swallowed this second one down. That's likely exactly how the food was made. From the sounds of it, however, a food allergy wasn't likely if he was eating the same types of things here as at home. "I'm going to request you undergo some allergy testing, but is there anything specifically you can think of that you had at home that you don't have here?"

"Beer." Clement jerked his shoulders up and lowered them down slowly in an awkward shrug. "But I haven't even had any of that at home since the insomnia started. My doctor said alcohol could hinder proper sleep patterns. They have sweets here, but I don't eat them. Darlene and I gave up desserts when the doctor told us in the spring that her sugars were borderline and my cholesterol was high."

My spine went as straight as a table leg. High cholesterol. Like Russ. That meant he would also be taking medication the way Russ did. "Since you've been here, have you been receiving your cholesterol medication?"

He nodded. "The prison doc doles them out and makes sure you swallow them. I guess they don't want people storing them up."

My brain was slotting the pieces into place almost faster than I could get the words out. "Did you have to bring in your own medications, or how does that work?"

"Darlene brought my bottle to the police station when we were waiting for the bail hearing." His eyebrows drew down into a line level with his glasses. "Those ran out about the same time I came here, and the ones I take now come from the prison dispensary."

I could see the moment he figured out what I was thinking. His eyebrows jumped up and dropped down.

"You think it was my medicine," he said.

I thought it seemed like the most likely cause, but that presented us with a problem. Either his family doctor had prescribed him something that would create insomnia instead of managing his high cholesterol, or Darlene was swapping out his pills at home.

I wanted the doctor to seem more likely. It would destroy Clement to find out Darlene betrayed him and was trying to murder him. It wouldn't have been that difficult for the doctor to do it. Not really.

A pharmacist wouldn't know what the customer had been diagnosed with, only what they'd been prescribed. If the medication didn't come with dangerous side effects and didn't have potential negative interactions with something they were already taking, some pharmacists didn't even discuss them with the patient before handing them the medication. Any time I'd picked up something at the pharmacy, Saul told me he'd put paperwork in the bag explaining the medication and all the side effects and that I should call him if I had any questions.

The specialists Clement saw for insomnia wouldn't have seen his actual pills. They'd have only looked at the list of medications Clement wrote up himself. Clement would have written down the high cholesterol medication he thought he was on.

As soon as I got Clement to sign the medical release, I'd go to the pharmacy and find out from Saul exactly what Clement was prescribed. Then I'd know whether to investigate his doctor or Darlene.

I sent a text to Anderson's secretary to fax the forms to the prison. Anderson said I could assign her administrative tasks for this case if I needed to since we were co-counsel and he'd be receiving payment for the case the same as I would.

"I'll look into your medication. I have a couple of theories about how it might have happened if we're right, but I don't want to go into it right now in case I'm wrong. You need to keep this between us. Have you told Darlene your suspicion?"

Clement's hands were stretched out on top of the table, and he was staring at them like they didn't belong to him. He didn't answer my question.

"Clement?"

"If we're right, I killed Gordon."

17

*M*y heart did a funny, sickly flutter beat that made me feel queasy. I opened my mouth to object, but I couldn't. He was right. If someone was trying to kill Clement by inducing fatal insomnia, they'd also indirectly killed Gordon Albright. The odds that someone had killed Gordon and tried to frame Clement for it at the same time as someone was trying to kill Clement were unreasonably slim.

Unless Gordon and Clement had both angered the same person and the same person tried to kill them both?

Clement still stared down at his hands.

I tapped the table. "Look at me, okay?"

He brought his gaze up, but red ringed his eyes.

"We have to take this one step at a time. Can you think of anyone who might have had a grudge against both of you? Or were you ever both together and witnessed something unusual?"

"No. No one. Gordon and I spent so much time together at

work that we didn't socialize on weekends. When we did, he always came to my house, and it was just the three of us." Clement brought his hands up and pressed his fingers into his forehead, right above his eyebrows. "The only people we interacted with together were patrons of the museum, and we haven't had an altercation with anyone except for the occasional rowdy group of bored teenagers in the summers."

I highly doubted rowdy teenagers would have the patience or resources to plan two such complex crimes.

"What about strange interactions when you purchased something for the museum? Did you use a different supplier for anything?"

"Everything's been normal." Clement rubbed tiny circles into his forehead. "Why would the person who wanted to kill me also try to frame me for Gordon's death? They could have killed him and dumped him in the lake with a lot less risk of being caught." He shook his head. "I had to have been the one who killed Gordon."

"If we're right, I'll do my best to see you don't go to prison for murder. Assuming you're cured, you're not a danger to anyone, and someone did this to you. That person should be punished."

Clement gave the kind of nod that said he didn't entirely agree with me. His fingers stayed steepled onto his face.

The person who tampered with Clement's medicine could be charged with attempted murder at the very least, and depending on how strong a case I could make, potentially for Gordon's murder as well.

But that still wouldn't get Clement acquitted. Now that we were both accepting that Gordon was collateral damage, I'd have to first prove Clement's medications had been altered, then show that alteration caused his fatal insomnia, which caused a hallucination that resulted in Gordon's death. And, at the end of all that, hope I could find precedent for having Clement released. Given the unusual circumstances, it'd be a long shot.

First, I had to make sure he didn't tip off Darlene if she was involved somehow.

He hadn't responded to my question about whether he'd told her his suspicions or not. I didn't want to plant doubt in his mind about his wife unnecessarily. Their relationship was already going to have a hard-enough time recovering from Gordon's murder, and Darlene might not have been involved at all in Clement's condition.

"I think it'd be better if you didn't tell Darlene about this for now."

Clement rubbed the spot where his wedding ring normally sat. "You think she'll find it hard to believe that I wasn't faking this whole time? She might think I meant to kill Gordon."

The poor man. Believing he'd killed his best friend was bad enough. Believing he might lose his wife as well could send him into a depression. There was a reason the guards removed all items a person could hang themselves with in prison.

I didn't want to be a contributing factor to Clement heading down that path. That would be as bad as planting doubts about his wife prematurely.

"I was thinking more that we don't want to get her hopes up. It could be that this is a temporary respite from your condition and it'll return. Maybe no one tampered with your medication at all. Give me time to look into it first, okay?"

Clement seemed to like the idea that his condition might simply be in remission better than that Darlene might believe he'd faked his disease to create an out for murdering his friend. That was love, when a man preferred death over losing his wife. At least he hadn't guessed at my real motive for asking him not to tell Darlene. That spoke to his love for her as well.

I got his permission to enter his house and remove an old pill bottle if I needed to. From my visit to Darlene, I knew that, like so many people in Fair Haven, they didn't lock their doors. All I'd need to do was find a time when Darlene wasn't home. Clement provided that for me, too. Darlene did water aerobics three mornings a week at the Fair Haven pool, and she'd recently joined a knitting club that met once a week.

Once the guard brought the medical release forms and Clement signed them, I headed out.

The first thing I needed to do was establish when his medication had been tampered with so I knew whether to investigate Darlene or Clement's doctor for a possible motive. Hopefully I could somehow prove that his medication had been altered. If I couldn't, Clement would go to prison for murder, and when he got out, someone might still want to kill him.

Saul would be able to tell me what prescription was on file for Clement. I still wanted to tell him about Gordon Albright's house as well and how it was already set up for someone in a wheelchair. Once it was released, Leonard would no doubt sell it, and people tended to want to move a house they'd inherited quickly, which meant they often sold for less than they otherwise would have. After losing his chance to buy the pharmacy, hopefully learning about a house that was already wheelchair accessible would cheer him up a little.

I parked as near the door of Dr. Horton's Pharmacy as I could to avoid the biting wind and headed inside.

A middle-aged man with dark hair and thick-rimmed glasses stood behind the counter where I'd expected to find Saul.

I stuttered to a stop. Surely the new owner hadn't fired Saul, but he had been worried about reduced hours.

The man gave me a professional smile, the kind you knew was offered only because they thought they should and not because they felt it. "Are you picking up a prescription or dropping off?"

I rested my fingers on the edge of the counter. Without Saul here, I felt like I wasn't even in the same pharmacy. If I had been here to pick up a new prescription, I would have felt very unbalanced to not be able to speak to him. Though maybe Saul was still here and this man was simply another employee hired by the new owner to help carry the load. Saul did work ridiculous hours.

"I actually wanted to talk to Saul about something. Is he in today?"

"He's out for a funeral, unfortunately. His brother-in-law passed away."

Poor Saul. To lose a family member on top of everything else he'd been going through. He couldn't seem to catch a break, and this must have come as a shock. When I'd been in here last time, he hadn't said anything about his brother-in-law being sick. Though it might not have come up anyway. We'd only talked about his brother-in-law in relation to how he'd been a contributing factor in his sister's death. "Was it sudden?"

"I think so. Saul said he went into a diabetic coma and didn't wake up. You can ask me what you need to, or he should be back in next week, if you're more comfortable waiting."

Some people might not have understood why Saul would even attend his brother-in-law's funeral or need time off to grieve, but I did. I'd attended the funeral of a man who tried to kill me. There was a sense of closure that came from attending. It let you put things behind you in a way you couldn't otherwise—or at least, it had for me. When your life was in turmoil, any bit of closure you could get was a blessing. My suspicion was that Russ was also struggling now because he'd never found a way to get that closure. Convincing him of that, though, was another thing altogether.

Saul might find his brother-in-law's funeral dredged up a lot of old emotions. A week might not even be enough, and I couldn't wait.

I explained who I was and laid out the signed consent forms, leaving out why I needed access to Clement's prescriptions. That wasn't something anyone else needed to know.

He printed off a list of all the medications the pharmacy had dispensed to Clement over the past year. The only one on the list I recognized was penicillin.

I pointed at the other two. "Could you tell me what these are for?"

"That one is the shingles shot." He touched a finger down beside the single-dose prescription on the list, then slid his finger down alongside all the others, filled at monthly intervals. "And these are for high cholesterol."

The heaviness in my stomach was so intense that I felt like my feet must be sinking into the floor. He received a high cholesterol medication from the pharmacy. That meant they had to be switched afterward by someone with easy access to them. Only two people had that kind of access to Clement's house. One of them was dead. The other was his wife.

Since the police hadn't found a motive for Clement to want to kill Gordon, the reverse was true as well. There wasn't a clear reason Gordon would have wanted to kill Clement.

Which left Darlene.

Now all that was left for me to do was prove it.

$\mathcal{I}$f Saul had been working instead of the new pharmacist, I might have asked more questions about what medications could cause insomnia. I trusted Saul to keep it to himself. I wasn't going to ask his replacement.

The Fair Haven rumor mill had a stronger draw than gravity. Some of the things I'd heard since coming here shouldn't have been common knowledge. Even though pharmacists weren't supposed to share confidential information, this man might think a question about medications that could cause insomnia didn't apply. After all, it wasn't a question about my personal medications or Clement's personal medications.

A general question probably wasn't even covered under confidentiality. So if I asked, I'd have to trust in the discretion of a stranger. If he were a gossipmonger, asking him not to share would only convince him he had a tastier tidbit of news.

Even if he went home and only told his roommate or his wife

about how a lawyer came in today asking about medications that could cause insomnia, that could travel the Fair Haven network before I woke up. Right now, I didn't want to risk tipping anyone off to what I was doing.

I thanked the pharmacist and left, taking the printout of Clement's medications with me.

I checked my watch. Tonight was the night of Darlene's knitting club, so I had to be there shortly after she would need to leave if I didn't want to have to wait until she went swimming on Monday. In the meantime, I had to hurry or I was going to be late to my supper with Mark and Stacey to talk about how we could get Russ to take our concerns about his health seriously.

MARK WALKED ME OUT TO MY CAR AFTER SUPPER WITH STACEY, but he didn't let go of my hand once we got there. "Are you really okay with all of us trying to talk to Russ independently first before we do an intervention-style sit-down?"

I'd been outvoted in our little meeting. Stacey wasn't comfortable with confronting Russ as a group, which shouldn't have surprised me considering how she'd been raised. Her father was a shy, private man who'd worked hard throughout her childhood to keep her out of the Fair Haven rumor circuit.

Mark simply hadn't thought Russ would react well to it.

The agreement we'd come to was that we'd each find a time in the next week to speak to him privately and express our concerns.

The theory was that it should have a similar effect of an intervention without the potential for negative rebound from Russ.

"I'm really okay with it. I think Saul's advice was good in that Russ needs to hear it from more than just me, but I agree we need to adapt that general advice to take Russ' personality into account." I squeezed his hand. "Besides, if this doesn't work, we can always try it the other way later."

Mark leaned in for a kiss, and for a minute, I forgot how cold it was outside.

When we finally pulled apart, I wanted to snuggle back into the warmth of his arms. We were so close to our wedding now, only a few more months. "It'll be nice when we can go home together instead of going our separate ways."

Mark flashed me those dimples of his that I was sure I'd love until the day we died. "Did you want to go to The Burnt Toast for some dessert before we part ways?"

I did, but I couldn't. Supper ran longer than expected, and Darlene would already be on her way to her knitting club. If I didn't go now, I'd have to wait. "I'd like to, but I have to search my client's house while his wife is away."

Mark's hand clenched around mine. "Why would you need to do that?" There was an edge to his tone.

I'd been so caught up in wanting to solve this conundrum and help Clement that I hadn't thought this part of the plan through the way I normally would. Taking a step back and looking at it through Mark's eyes, perhaps it wasn't wise to go in alone. Even though I didn't think Darlene would hurt me if she found me there—if she was guilty, she chose a very non-confrontational way to kill Clement—it was better not to take that chance at all.

I explained the situation to him. "I could use some backup. You can drop me off and then park somewhere along the road. If I'm not out before you spot Darlene's car coming back, you can call me to let me know to get out. What do you think?"

"What are my chances of convincing you not to go at all?"

"Slim to none. It's the only way for me to figure out if my client's wife was trying to kill him."

"Then I suppose I'll have to play Robin to your Batman again, because you know I'm not letting you go alone."

I felt a lot less like Batman than like a cat burglar, but Clement had given me permission to go into his home and look for old pill bottles. And having Mark back as my sidekick on a crazy scheme reminded me of how we'd hunted for my Uncle Stan's killer together.

Which unfortunately brought another idea to mind. It was possible Clement's medications were the medications he'd been prescribed and that something else had been crushed up and put into his food at home. That'd been the case in one of my earliest investigations in Fair Haven, and it would also explain why Clement got better in prison since he'd stopped eating food from his own home.

If Darlene did that, I likely wouldn't ever be able to prove it. I had to pray she hadn't been that crafty. It'd have been much simpler for her to swap out the medications and allow Clement to harm himself without realizing it.

Clement had said he started sleeping after he ran out of the medication Darlene brought him from home. My original theory still seemed stronger than my new one. We wouldn't know until I found a pill bottle.

On the drive there, I described the Dodds' car to Mark as best I could remember it.

He let me off at the house. "Should I call or text when I see her car?"

A text would be less intrusive, but it could take too long. I'd have to have time to get to the back door and out into the woods before she entered the house or she might see me. "Call."

I waved goodbye and walked right in the front door. With the way our world was going, I didn't see how people still felt safe leaving their doors unlocked. I could have been someone intending to rob them or lie in wait and hurt Darlene as easily as I was Clement's lawyer looking for evidence.

I got my phone out of my pocket—I left my purse in the car with Mark—so I would be able to answer immediately.

I moved slowly deeper into the house.

All the lights were off. As Mark pulled away down the driveway, darkness closed in on me, tight and heavy. My breathing shallowed, and I struggled to take deep enough breaths to keep from getting lightheaded. Now that I was living in Fair Haven permanently, I should consider petitioning them for more street lights.

I'd expected Darlene would leave a light on. I hated coming home to a dark, empty house, even though my dogs were there, so I always left the front light on and a light inside. Turning a light on in her house wasn't an option. It'd be too obvious if she made it to the end of her driveway before I could turn it off after Mark called. I should have brought a flashlight.

My shin connected with something hard, my phone shot out of my hand, and I yelped. I bent over and rubbed the sore spot. Good thing they didn't have a dog. I'd be dinner right about now.

Though I now had a bigger problem than becoming doggie chow. My phone was somewhere in the dark. I got down on my hands and knees and groped along the floor. I'd be in a real spot if Mark called before I found it. I'd have wasted all my time and gotten nothing to show for it. But at least it would light up if he called and I'd be able to find it.

Light up. I smacked my forehead. My phone had a built-in flashlight. If I could find it.

It felt like ten minutes passed before my eyes adjusted, and I spotted my phone wedged under the corner of the couch. I'd run my shin into their coffee table.

I swooped my phone up and turned on my cellphone light.

I made my way through the living room, giving the door into the office where Gordon died a wide berth. I'd check the kitchen first. Some people kept their medications there because they took them with breakfast.

The table and counters were clear of anything except a jar of peanut butter and a crumb-covered plate with a knife resting across it. Had Darlene eaten only peanut butter toast for supper? I knew it wasn't left over from breakfast because I could still smell the warm yeasty aroma of toasting bread in the air. Maybe she'd been too short on time to cook.

Or...she'd told me Clement and Gordon cooked breakfast every morning. Not every woman, even of Darlene's generation, was a good cook or liked to cook. If Clement was the cook in the household, it definitely meant Darlene hadn't been seeding his food with anything that could cause insomnia.

If he took care of so much, the little lawyer's voice in my head whispered, *why would she want to kill him?*

It was a question I couldn't answer now. First I had to find evidence that she had before I looked for the reasons why.

I opened each cupboard and the drawers. No pill bottles. Clement said he only took the one medication, so he didn't use the weekly pill dispenser that my Uncle Stan used to have.

If the pills weren't in the kitchen, that left Clement and Darlene's bedroom and bathrooms. I'd used their powder room during my brief visit to see Darlene. It was a pedestal sink with no medicine chest or other storage in the room where someone would keep medications.

I went back the way I'd come and crossed to the other side of the house. Presumably that's where the bedrooms and full bathroom were since I hadn't seen them yet.

The first door I opened must have been a bedroom in a prior life. Now it was stacked full of boxes, a lantern, and a two-man logging saw that had to be at least five feet tall.

Clement's meds wouldn't be in there unless he wanted to lose them.

I opened the next door. Bingo. Master bedroom. The door off the other side must lead into their bathroom. I'd check there first.

I looked on the sink, in the vanity under the sink, and in the medicine chest. No pill bottles belonging to Clement. This might have been a fool's errand. Most people threw away empty medicine bottles as soon as they took the last dose, and the bathroom garbage had clearly been emptied recently. If there'd been an empty bottle here, it would have been gone over a month ago since Darlene left the most recent bottle at the Fair Haven police station for Clement.

I needed to look for bottles that would still be here after a month. The only trash can in my house that didn't get emptied often was the one in the bedroom.

I shone my light around the room. A trash can huddled next to the dresser. I went over and nudged it with my foot. A couple of tissues, an empty tube of hand cream, and a mint wrapper.

Darlene had to be almost done at her knitting club. I didn't know how far away it was. Just because I'd never heard of a knitting club in Fair Haven didn't mean there wasn't one. Knitting wasn't exactly my thing. I'd have likely taken an eye out with the needles.

All I could hope was that her club was in a nearby town instead. At least Mark hadn't called me yet.

I tapped my foot. If I were a pill bottle, where would I hide?

Smart, Nikki. If you were a pill bottle, you wouldn't hide anywhere because you wouldn't be a sentient being.

So if I were someone who took medication, and I kept it in my bedroom, where might I drop a bottle if I didn't want to cross the room to throw it out? My Uncle Stan used to keep his medications in the drawer of his bedside table.

I pulled open the drawer of one bedside table. Ladies reading glasses and a romance novel lay inside. That drawer must belong to Darlene.

One last chance. I'd check the other bedside table, and then I'd leave, even if Mark hadn't called. If it wasn't here, I was out of ideas, and Darlene could be home any moment.

Clement's drawer stuck. The force of my pull rattled the bed stand, and a shiver raced down my chest. I glanced automatically over my shoulder toward the door. I needed to get out of here. I was starting to get jumpy, my heart beating so loud I might not have been able to hear the door open over it.

After all, what did I really expect Mark to do if Darlene caught me here somehow and wanted to kill me? It's not like he was in the house with me.

I wriggled the drawer more gently, and it slid open. An empty pill bottle rolled to the front.

Finally.

I grabbed it out and shoved the door tightly closed. Hopefully there'd be enough residue inside that I could get it tested by a lab to determine what'd been in it.

A creak came from the front of the house, and then the front door banged shut.

19

I almost lost my grip on both my phone and the pill bottle. My fingers shook so hard I missed hitting the spot to turn my cell phone light off the first time I tried.

The screen still glowed, though. Darlene would see it—and me—if she came back to this part of the house. Why hadn't Mark called to warn me?

If he thought he saw Darlene's car now, he'd call and give me away. I turned my phone off and jammed it into my pocket.

I had to get out. Maybe I could sneak past Darlene.

I tiptoed to the door and strained to hear. Her footsteps were coming toward me. The whapping noise sounded like she'd exchanged her shoes for heel-less slippers.

There'd be no way I could explain snooping around her bedroom in the dark. She'd know I was looking for something I didn't want to tell her about, and if she had hurt Clement, she'd make sure any evidence of it was gone. Tipping off a person you were investigating was one of the worst things that could happen.

I could make a break for it and hope she didn't recognize me, but that seemed unlikely. She'd probably turned on at least one light in the main part of the house. Besides, she'd call the police to report a break-in and my fingerprints were all over the place. I could argue to the police that I'd been in the house previously, but Darlene would still guess I might have been the one. That brought me right back to tipping her off if she was the guilty party.

The only other door in the room led into the bathroom. Hiding in the bathroom wouldn't work, either. With my luck, she was heading this way to get ready for bed.

Bed! Could I fit under the bed?

It was a canopy style, so it didn't rest flat on the ground. Assuming Darlene and Clement hadn't stored too much stuff under there, I might be able to wiggle in.

I dropped to my belly and slid in sideways, my head at the head of the bed and my feet at the feet. The lights flared on. I froze. My body was completely underneath the bed, but I'd planned to move farther back from the edge. Right now, if I moved too much, she'd likely be able to spot the motion.

I wished she'd left the lights off for another reason, too. They illuminated everything else that was under the bed with me, including a balled-up sock, some rumpled tissues, and a lot of dust and cobwebs. At least it was good to know I wasn't the only person who regularly forgot to clean under the bed.

Darlene's slipper-covered feet—they were blue and looked a bit like she was wearing an 80s shag carpet—moved past the bed and toward the bathroom. Seemed like I'd made the right call not to hide in there. If she filled the tub, I might be able to escape while she was bathing.

The sound of water running started, but it was too small for the tub, more like the sink tap.

A tingle tickled my nose.

Do not sneeze, I mentally chanted to myself. *Don't do it.*

I'd heard somewhere that if you pressed a finger to the pressure point under your nose it would stop a sneeze. I'd never tried it before, but I wasn't going to be able to hold it in much longer without some sort of help. I eased my hand up from my side.

My fingers brushed a cylindrical shape. It rolled away from me with a rattle, and my body forgot that it wanted to sneeze and give away my hiding place. That felt like another pill container. One with an actual pill in it.

I stretched my arm back and out until my shoulder screamed at me. I had to reach it. Quietly. The running water from the tap had hopefully covered the sound it made, but it wouldn't cover the noise of me whacking a body part off the underside of the bed trying to reach it.

My fingers connected a second time. I strained an extra half an inch and closed my pointer and middle finger around the bottle like pinchers. I brought it up to my face. It was a pill bottle, and it looked like at least one pill was still inside, maybe two.

Clement must have dropped it accidentally and hadn't been able to find it again. Being that close to the end of the bottle, he'd likely simply called in a refill rather than bothering to waste too much time hunting for it.

Now all I had to do was get it, and myself, out of here.

The tap in the bathroom stopped running, and Darlene's footfalls approached the bed.

My body felt like it was trembling from the inside out, all my organs processing too fast, like I'd had twice the amount of coffee I normally drink. She couldn't possibly know I was here, right?

Her footsteps turned into shuffles. The bed above me squeaked, and her feet disappeared.

Not good. Almost worse than her finding me here. She was crawling into bed, presumably to read, since she hadn't turned off the lights.

I couldn't lay here all night. I couldn't even lay here for another hour. My body would cramp up, forcing me to move—which she'd hear—or I'd sneeze from the dust—which she'd most definitely hear. And I'd stupidly turned my phone off. There was no way to turn it back on and text Mark for help without her hearing me.

This is why lawyers don't break into houses and hide under beds, Nicole, I could almost hear my mom saying.

If I was in a movie, I'd throw something across the room and the bad guy would fall for it and think someone was where my item hit. Sadly, I doubted that would work in real life. I might be trapped here a very long time.

I tracked the minutes ticking by on my watch. A half hour passed, and the cramp in my lower back felt like I'd been run over by a lawnmower. Mark had undoubtedly tried to call me by now, and was probably panicking over the fact that my phone would be going straight to voicemail.

Maybe if I moved quietly and stayed low to the ground, I could crawl out of the room without her noticing me. She might have already drifted off or be so engrossed in what she was reading that she wouldn't catch the motion out of the corner of her eye.

I inched closer to the edge of the bed. I shifted my leg out first, and then reached out with my arm.

The doorbell rang, and I wedged myself backward as fast as I could.

Darlene got up off the bed. I wasn't fast enough. As she came around the end, my shoe still stuck out. I laid as still as possible, even holding my breath.

She didn't look to the side or down. Thank you, Lord.

This was my chance. I didn't know where the door on the other side of the hall led, but it had to be better than staying under the bed. Worst case, it went into another bedroom, and I'd be trapped there until Darlene fell soundly asleep.

I wriggled out as quickly as I could without making too much noise and picked my way across the floor to the bedroom door. I'd wait until she actually answered the door before I made my break for it. That way I could be certain of where she was.

It felt like it took her twice the normal time to cross the house. Or maybe she'd been at the door for a while and was checking the peephole before opening it. For a moment, I wondered if she locked the door while she was home alone, even though she didn't lock it when she was away.

"Can I help you?" Darlene's voice carried from a distance.

"I'm the county medical examiner."

My feet stopped working for a second. What was Mark doing here? He seemed to be speaking at twice his normal volume.

Then my brain caught up. He was here because he was worried about me. If Darlene had me tied up somewhere, he wanted me to hear him and make noise to let him know where I was.

I wouldn't be doing that. Thankfully, his arrival gave me the distraction I needed.

I scurried across the hall while Mark was telling Darlene he needed to confirm what temperature they kept the house at because it influenced time of death. And could she tell him where the heat sources were?

The source of the heat didn't matter, but Darlene wouldn't know that, and the longer Mark kept her talking, the better.

I eased open the door across the hall, silently praying it wasn't a windowless storage room.

On the other side was their garage, and in it sat the car I'd seen before. No wonder Mark hadn't called to warn me. I hadn't realized the Dodds had two cars.

Before Mark ran out of things to say, I slipped through the door and closed it behind me. Then I ran to the door that led outside.

My car was parked in such a way that I couldn't climb into the passenger seat. I'd have to crawl into the back on the driver's side.

I did a hunched run along the edge of the garage and sprinted the two steps through the open space between it and my car. As soon as I hit the back bumper, I squatted down and frog-walked to where I could reach the door handle. Thank goodness no one was around to see this.

I opened the door just wide enough for me to crawl into the back, onto the floor. The overhead light blinked on, but there was nothing I could do about that. Hopefully Darlene was distracted enough by Mark's questions that she didn't notice.

Having to keep hidden meant I couldn't watch for Mark to return. I'd only been in the car for around thirty seconds when the driver's side door opened and Mark slid in.

He hit his fist into the steering wheel and pulled out his phone, presumably to call me.

"Don't turn around," I whispered.

He cursed softly. "I was worried she'd chopped you up with one of the museum axes and hid your body parts in buckets in the basement."

"I think that only happens in horror movies." I shifted around, but couldn't get comfortable. Whoever designed cars with that weird bump in the middle of the backseat floor clearly hadn't considered how it would feel if someone needed to lay on it. "Besides, they don't have a basement as far as I could see."

Mark put the car into drive. "You're not nearly as funny as you think you are," he said, but he couldn't completely hide the smile in his voice. "How did you get into the car?"

As he drove us to the nearest safe place to stop outside of Darlene's view, I told him exactly what had happened.

By the time he stopped and I swapped positions into the front passenger's seat, he was laughing outright. "I might not believe that story unless I saw the cobweb in your hair."

"What?" I swiped a hand over my hair and it really did come away with sticky web tendrils on it. I shuddered. "At least I got the pill bottle, and I managed to find one with a couple pills left in it."

"Did you check the date? We don't know how long ago he lost them under the bed."

Arg. He was right. I turned my cell phone light back on and shone it on the bottle. The date on the one I'd found under the bed said it was two months old, so it was well within the range of time when Clement had been suffering from what the doctors thought was fatal insomnia.

Tomorrow I'd work on figuring out what the pills were. Tonight, all I was going to do was get a shower to make sure there weren't any spiders nesting in my hair.

or the rest of the night, even after my shower, I kept jumping, feeling like something was crawling on me. I slept terribly because I had two separate nightmares about spiders coming up from under my bed to crawl on me. When I woke up from the second nightmare, I dragged the vacuum up the stairs and cleaned underneath my bed.

By the time I finished, I couldn't fall back asleep. The clock told me it was 6:30 am. Even though I wouldn't have dropped in on anyone else that early, Russ would have been up for at least half an hour already.

I didn't want to take the pills to anyone for analysis until I'd confirmed that they weren't the medication they were supposed to be. Clement's next court date was rapidly approaching. If the pill in the bottle was exactly what it was supposed to be, I didn't want to waste time chasing mirages under the assumption they were going to give us something we could use. Since Russ took the same medication, I could compare what I'd found to his.

Velma and Toby's tails rattled their crates when they heard my footsteps on the stairs. I fed them, suited them up in the extra-large winter doggie coats I'd bought them, and took them with me. Russ always enjoyed a visit from the dogs, so they might as well come along.

The ground outside was covered in one of the extra-thick frost layers that I hadn't known existed until I moved to Michigan. Looking out the window and seeing it covering the leaves and barren tree branches, it looked almost like a light dusting of snow, but it wasn't. By the time the sun came up, it would vanish except for in the shadows, and by noon it'd be completely gone. As they sniffed along the path on our walk, Velma and Toby's breath came out white, like they had fires lit in their bellies.

Russ answered the door, already dressed in the jeans and flannel shirt that seemed to be his uniform as soon as the weather turned. The house smelled like eggs, bacon, and wood smoke. My mouth watered, but it wasn't the best breakfast for someone trying to look good in her wedding dress...or someone who was already on high cholesterol and high blood pressure meds.

"Come on in." His smile lacked the Santa Claus sparkle I'd come to expect. "Word of advice. Don't read the obituaries over breakfast. It's depressing when you see so many people who've died who are your age and younger."

Maybe I could make this trip serve a dual purpose and take my turn speaking to Russ about my fears for his health.

I let the dogs loose once we were inside the door. "Anyone you know?"

"Two people I went to school with. Victor Kristoffersen and Edna Orr. Edna was two years younger. Always fit. She even used to be on the girls' swim team. She went of a heart attack, and Victor died of a stroke." He sank into his chair and looked up at me. "You wouldn't know Edna. She moved a couple towns over after she got married, but Victor owned the pharmacy. I should go to both their funerals and pay my respects to the families."

I knew the name sounded familiar. That was from where. So even if Victor had kept his word to Saul, Saul wouldn't have gotten the chance to purchase the business from Victor, though maybe whoever inherited it from Victor might have still given him a fair deal. It was a moot point now. The pharmacy was sold before Victor's death.

Russ' plate still had two pieces of buttered toast and a slice of bacon on it. He shoved the bacon into his mouth and chewed, but it was almost like he wasn't paying attention. "Makes you think."

I dragged a chair close to his and put a hand on his shoulder. "Makes me think about how I don't want to lose you early, too."

Russ wagged a piece of toast at me. "I'll tell you what I told Stacey when she made a fuss about a tiny bit of tightness in my chest—I'm fine."

How did you convince someone who didn't see the way they were sabotaging themselves? Everyone around Russ could see how he was hurting himself and where he'd be headed if he didn't start taking better care of his health. He didn't.

I wasn't sure how to convince him—how any of us, together or separately, would be able to convince him. Everything I could think to say was a regurgitation of conversations we'd had before.

I pulled the pill bottle from my purse instead. "I'm working a case where we think a medication might have been swapped out. I need a bit of help."

Russ set aside his toast. "You're not getting yourself involved in something dangerous again, are you? I've also been thinking I was wrong to encourage you to go back to being a lawyer. Working at Sugarwood is safer."

If I wasn't careful, he wouldn't let me see his pills at all. From my very first investigation into Uncle Stan's death, Russ hadn't liked me poking around in what he considered private business and drawing attention to myself from dangerous people.

He shoved back his chair and waddled to the counter. He poured another cup of coffee, and added milk and sugar to it. It had to be for me. He took his black.

He dropped it down in front of me, and the coffee splashed out onto his table. "You can't just think about yourself anymore either. Think about Mark."

This conversation was not supposed to be about me or about me and Mark. It was supposed to be about Russ' health and Clement's pills. Somehow I'd lost control of it.

Russ added another swipe of butter to his cold toast. The knife hopped across the surface of the bread instead of drawing across smoothly, like he was taking his frustration at me out on the poor toast slice.

And then I understood. What he said was *think about Mark*. What he meant was *I can't stand to lose anyone else.*

Maybe Russ knew on some level what he was doing to his health, but he didn't care because eating made him feel better for a little while. Eating was a classic way to try to deal with emotional pain. I knew it because I was a stress and emotional eater. That wasn't a healthy way to deal with stress and grief and disappointment, but it was the easiest one, especially if you weren't sure what else to do.

Russ had lost so many people, both in the past and more recently. I understood what that did to you. I was afraid of losing him, too.

Maybe we'd been approaching his health from the wrong direction. If his physical health reflected his mental health, then maybe that was where we needed to start.

Problem was, I didn't know how to get there. Russ came from an era that didn't understand mental health and felt that needing to see a therapist was a weakness.

But he was worried about me. Maybe that could be our first step. He might be more open to the idea if I made it about me and Stacey needing help. She'd asked me last week about whether I found my counseling sessions helpful. She'd been considering seeing someone.

"Mark and I have talked about my safety a lot." We'd actually talked about it months ago, and we'd come to a workable agreement for both of us. Russ didn't need to know that. He also didn't need to know that I hadn't been taking risks intentionally, consciously or otherwise. "I've always found it easier to deal with grief by acting, and so that might have made me take more risks than I should have. I don't want anyone to wonder what really happened to their loved one. Stacey does it, too, working even when she should be resting because that's how she's been dealing with Noah's death. Maybe we both need a little more support, like a grief group or something."

Russ was nodding along with me.

"Would you…" I dropped my gaze to the coffee cup as if it were hard for me to ask. I hated to trick him the way I did suspects, but it was better than him dying within the next few years. "Would you come with us?"

Keeping my gaze down was more challenging than not asking *What is it?* when someone says *I have a secret.* But I wasn't used to exercising my interviewing skills on a friend. If I didn't continue to stare at my mug of coffee, my expression might give something away.

Russ picked up his empty plate and dropped it in the sink with a clank. "Okay." Then, as if he were worried I might continue the conversation by asking him about his own feelings, he sat back at the table with me and grabbed the pill bottle I'd set there. "Now what is this you needed my help with?"

"I needed a way—a safe way," I added quickly, "to tell whether the pills in this bottle are what the bottle says they are. Since you take the same thing, all I need to do is compare them with yours."

"You can look at any of my medicines you want if it keeps you from talking to people you shouldn't be."

Russ went to the cupboard over his sink and brought down a green plastic pill bottle. He popped the top and shook four of them out onto the table. The pills were white and oval shaped.

I gently opened Clement's pill bottle. With how clumsy I was, I had images of me removing the top too forcefully, sending the pill shooting across the room, and losing it down the drain in Russ' sink.

I tapped the bottle until one of the two pills slid out into the lid.

It was a yellowish-orange shade and round.

No one could confuse the two pills. I had one more thing I needed to check—the information on the two bottles. It had to match. Otherwise, the difference in color could be a dosage indicator. That wouldn't explain the difference in shape, though. Brand might, if one of them took the name brand and one took a generic brand. Russ took generic medications to save money.

I held out my hand, and Russ passed me his bottle. I laid them side by side on the table.

The dosage and brand name were exact.

Someone had swapped out Clement's pills.

took Velma and Toby home the long way through the woods. My mind worked the case, and if I'd gone directly home, I would have ended up pacing the house.

Darlene wanting to kill Clement made no sense. Clement adored Darlene. He'd taken care of her. What could have possibly motivated her to want to kill a man who, by all evidence, was good and kind and loved her?

If I had any hope of having Clement's charge reduced or dropped, I needed a strong argument and a lot of proof that his suddenly cured medical condition had been real and had been inflicted by someone else. Without a clear motive, that'd be difficult.

I walked until my nose turned so cold that it hurt. I must have kept us out longer than I thought, because when we got home, both dogs dropped immediately to their beds for a nap.

With them quiet, I pulled out all the material I'd collected. Most of it related to Gordon and wasn't applicable anymore. As much as I hated to admit it, Clement must have been the one to kill Gordon.

I set aside everything that applied to Gordon. All that was left was the background checks that Hal, the private investigator who regularly worked for Anderson's firm, ran for me on Clement and Darlene when he got back from his vacation, the newspaper article about the opening of the museum that I'd printed off, and what Clement told me about their life.

Both background checks were unexceptional. No extra money spent. No outstanding debts. The Dodds were average, responsible people. They'd saved for their retirement, and all their current income came from Clement's early retirement pension from teaching and the museum. They'd inherited their home and the museum from Clement's dad, so they didn't even have a mortgage.

I wasn't going to get anywhere staring at the same material I'd read multiple times. My brain had already fallen into repeating patterns. My dad always warned new hires about it. You only got one chance to see material fresh, he said.

I'd been blinded by what we thought happened. We thought this was either a horrible accident brought on by a naturally occurring medical condition or that someone had targeted Gordon. That someone had targeted Clement instead hadn't even entered my mind.

I wasn't going to be able to see the material fresh again, so the best alternative was to instead find fresh material.

I called Hal and asked him to put a tail on Darlene for a week. It might end up being a waste of resources, but I didn't know where else to start. I also started work on a subpoena for Darlene's cell phone records.

A knock sounded at my door. Hopefully it wasn't Russ ready to back out of the grief support group meeting already. If he did, I was out of ideas for how to help him.

Stacey stood outside my door instead, a bundled-up stroller behind her on the ground. Since she said Noah was sleeping, we carried the stroller up together, took the blanket off, and left him the way he was even though what I really wanted to do was take him out and snuggle him.

But Stacey was twisting a strand of her hair around her finger before we had the door closed and Noah settled. With Stacey, that was never a good sign.

Russ wouldn't have called her as soon as I left to talk to her about how much she needed a grief group, would he? If that was it, I'd better jump in and tell her what I'd done before she started the conversation. Otherwise, she could feel like I'd betrayed her somehow and was talking about her behind her back.

"I had an idea about Russ," I blurted out.

I forced my words to slow down so I didn't sound so guilt-ridden and filled her in as I made us both a cup of chamomile tea. I would have rather had coffee, but Stacey was off coffee because of Noah, and it seemed callous to drink it in front of her.

Stacey gave a doesn't-matter shrug. "Those are usually free, so it's probably a good place for me to start, too."

Her nonchalant attitude made it seem like she hadn't known and that wasn't why she came. Yet she kept shifting position in her seat. It made her look a bit like she really needed to use the restroom.

She finally stilled on her seat. "Have you decided whether you're going back to being a lawyer?"

Technically, I'd never stopped, but I knew what she meant. She wanted to know what I'd decided about joining Anderson's practice. That shouldn't have made her nervous, but it seemed like it did. "I'm waiting to make my decision until I've had to argue the current case in court."

If I couldn't manage a case on my own, it wasn't right of me to take on clients at all. I'd willingly help Anderson as a consultant whenever he had an innocent client, but I couldn't sign clients if I couldn't see their case through to the end. It wasn't fair to them to pass them off when they were at their most vulnerable.

Besides, despite what Saul said, it wasn't enough to love a career. You also needed to be good at it. If I couldn't competently do all aspects of my job, I needed to move on to a new one. That's what responsible grown-ups did, like it or not.

Stacey had a ring of hair around her finger, and she held it up by her cheek like she wished she could chew on it. With anyone else, I would have simply asked what was going on. With Stacey, I had to approach it a bit more tactfully.

"Are you planning something that we might need to do around here before more of my time would be taken up by the practice?"

Even though Stacey wasn't supposed to be working during her maternity leave, we hadn't been able to keep her from unofficially continuing to involve herself in almost everything that came up. She and Nancy had designed the whole new product line for the website and for sale in the Short Stack, our pancake house. Nancy would handle all the baking, but Stacey was the organizational genius.

Stacey shook her head. "It's just that..." She brushed her hair against her lips, seemed to notice what she was doing, and dropped the lock. "I need to make a decision about where I'm going to work once my mat leave is over."

The chair suddenly felt wobbly underneath me. I wanted to beg Stacey to stay at Sugarwood—literally get down on my knees and offer her whatever it took. All the paperwork and inventory maintenance that Stacey loved required twice the day's normal allotment of caffeine and more candy than I should eat over the course of two weeks for me to face.

But it wasn't right of me to say any of that or to pressure her. If I did, I'd be like everyone else who tried to control her life rather than letting her figure out on her own what she wanted. Besides, any time someone pushed Stacey, she inevitably wanted to go in the opposite direction.

I stopped my mental panic hamster wheel. She'd opened this wanting to know what I planned to do. "I don't see the link."

She huffed like it was obvious and I was being intentionally obtuse, making her say something that she didn't want to say. "If you're staying on full-time at Sugarwood, then there won't be a position for me. Since I'm not doing all the jobs Noah did, I can't expect you to pay me a full-time wage for part-time equipment maintenance. And I need full-time income to support Noah and me."

She sounded defensive. So much so that I almost missed the little break in her voice when she said *for me*.

She wasn't defensive. She was defending herself from the disappointment of not having a place here. She'd decided she wanted to stay, but now that I wasn't moving to DC—wasn't even sure I'd continue practicing law—she thought I'd want to take back the roles at Sugarwood that I'd handed over to her.

Even if I went back to working at Sugarwood full-time, I wouldn't want to take back those jobs. "You have a job here no matter what I choose. I thought you knew that."

Stacey shook her head, opened her mouth as if she were going to say something, and then shook her head again.

My heart hurt a little with every beat over the thought that she'd been sitting at home worrying over this. Russ and I agreed we wouldn't talk to Stacey about the job again until she was ready because we didn't want her to feel pressured. It seemed that had been a mistake.

Stacey wasn't a hugger, so I didn't try even though I wanted to. "We've been afraid you didn't want to work here anymore. Both Russ and I want you here, training to take over for him someday, no matter what I decide. Okay?"

Stacey dipped her head. "Then I'd like the job. I'd like to stay here at Sugarwood."

We ate cookies and chatted about other things for another half hour. Before Stacey left, I couldn't help myself. I had to hold Noah for a few minutes.

Until he arrived, I hadn't had much experience with babies, and I hadn't understood what people meant when they said it was love at first sight with their kids. If I felt this way about Noah, I could only imagine what it would be like when Mark and I had our own children.

It felt like the breath had been sucked from my body. Maybe that was why Darlene tried to kill Clement. Their son. Clement had likely been with him during the fishing trip when he died. He was too young in the photos to have gone alone.

It was possible Darlene blamed Clement for their son's death and hadn't been able to take it anymore.

22

I passed the next few days working with Nancy and Stacey to get the new items up on the website, collecting all Clement's medical records from the specialists he'd seen who'd diagnosed him with fatal insomnia, and researching everything I could find on the condition.

I focused on other cases where people with fatal insomnia had exhibited hallucinations. There wasn't much information. The condition was so rare. I was able to find a neurologist in New York who'd studied the condition and had published scholarly articles on the topic. He'd agreed to testify if I needed him.

Whether I liked it or not, my trial by fire to see if I should join Anderson in his practice or investigate a new career was turning out to be a case that would have challenged even my parents in the courtroom.

But assuming I could prove that Clement's condition had been genuine, I might have figured out a way to keep Clement out of prison. There'd been a sleep-walking case a few years ago where a man believed he was fighting with an intruder and accidentally killed his wife. It was so similar to Clement's case that I could argue it set a precedent for finding Clement not guilty.

This afternoon, I planned to go back to the pharmacy since Saul should have returned to work by now. I wanted him to identify the medications in Clement's pill bottle. Once I knew what they were, I'd find another expert I could call to the stand to confirm that the pills substituted for Clement's could cause severe insomnia.

I was on my way to the car to head to Dr. Horton's when my cell phone rang.

"I have pictures for you, Ms. Fitzhenry-Dawes," Hal said. "The lady you asked me to tail met twice with the same guy, and they looked awfully friendly. You want to come pick physical copies up or you want me to email you the files."

Awfully friendly was a euphemism for *might be having an affair.*

I'd been wondering why Darlene would have waited so long to punish Clement if she blamed him for the death of their son. Perhaps it was because she was so dependent on Clement. It was possible she'd been afraid of being on her own. If she'd found someone to take Clement's place, that could explain why she'd finally acted on a desire to punish her husband for not protecting their child.

I tapped my phone softly against my cheek. We were only a weekend away from Clement's preliminary hearing. The best idea seemed to be for me to take a picture of the man to Clement today and see if he recognized him in case it was a family member.

I couldn't afford to waste time investigating this if it turned out he was Darlene's cousin or something, consoling with her because her husband was in prison on the charge of murder. I had told her it would be good if she had someone to lean on. She might have called a relative.

If I was showing them to Clement, or later to Darlene to confront her, a larger image than I could bring up on my phone would serve better. I still didn't want to let Clement know I suspected Darlene, though. "I'll come get them from you. Did you get any pictures of the man alone?"

"A couple when he was getting back in his car."

"Do you have his name yet?"

"Naw. Be nice if he offered it up, but he didn't, and I stuck with my tail instead of following him."

Technically the right call, but frustrating none the less. "See what you can do for me, okay?"

"Sure thing."

I arranged to meet him in twenty minutes since his office wasn't in Fair Haven. It meant postponing my trip to the pharmacy, but Saul wasn't going anywhere, and this could be the lead that finally solved this puzzle. Even knowing what the pills were meant nothing if I didn't have a motive to show why they'd been put there intentionally and maliciously.

Before I left his office, I looked through the pictures. They didn't clear up whether the man Darlene had met with was a lover or a friend. He hadn't gotten any shots of them holding hands or kissing, but they'd met twice in the span of a week. Hal had taken a couple shots of them hugging.

I headed straight for the prison. If Clement didn't recognize the man, our next step would be figuring out who he was.

I left all but one clear shot of the man's face in my car. Soon I'd need to tell Clement what I suspected, but I couldn't gauge what would happen when I did. Some men, when faced with their wife's infidelity or sabotage, turned angry. Others sank into depression. If he ended up going to prison for life for the murder of his best friend because of something his beloved wife did, I was afraid of what he might do to himself.

When I sat across the table from Clement, his leg jiggled so hard that the table had a slight vibration to it like we were sitting next to train tracks with a train going by.

"I didn't expect to see you again before the arraignment." He moved a hand under the table, and the jittering stopped as if he were holding his leg still. "Has something new happened?"

I handed him the photo. "I'm following every lead I can. Do you recognize this man?"

Clement brought the photo close to him and stared at it. There was no twitch of recognition. His expression didn't shift at all—no extra swallowing, no downward pull on his lips, no tensing of his eye muscles. Nothing.

But he kept looking at it long enough that I wanted to start squirming in my seat. I might have if I hadn't heard my mom's voice in my head. *Don't ever show a client that you're uncomfortable.*

He set the picture down and brought his other hand back up, but his leg stayed still. He didn't push the photo back to me the way I expected he would. "I don't know him."

His look made me feel like I was being sized up, as if I were a child in the principal's office, called in to defend against a charge of cheating.

I kept my mouth shut. Defending against an unspoken accusation would only make me seem guiltier of whatever he thought I'd done.

He laid a hand over top of the picture as if he were tired of looking at it. "I've been sitting here trying to think of all the possible reasons you would show me a picture of a man I don't know. Because if I don't know him, he shouldn't have had access to my medications or a reason to hurt me."

The sleep-deprived Clement had been easier to manage. The well-rested Clement showed me the man who must have been a sharp professor and history scholar in the past. This conversation had taken a turn to a direction I'd hoped to avoid.

He was going to want to talk about who this man was and why I was asking about him. All the factors I'd calculated meant nothing because I'd failed to take into account how much sharper Clement would be now. In his career, he'd had to take small pieces of evidence—the things artifacts told him—and come to conclusions about whole societies and eras of history. It wasn't that much different from what I did in a way. We used a similar interpretive skill set.

He flexed and relaxed his hand over the photo. "So the one reason I can come up with is that you think Darlene is having an affair with this man and she swapped out my medication to kill me."

I couldn't deny it, and I couldn't grasp on to another idea that might distract him. My ruse was up. At this point, I was probably better admitting it. Then I could minimize the damage and hopefully keep Clement calm and focused. To build a solid defense for him, I needed his cooperation.

I straightened into my most professional posture. "Yes, that's what I suspect."

"Did Darlene admit to having an affair?"

"I haven't asked her yet."

The lines in his forehead deepened until they were almost as thick as his glasses' rims. "Do you have pictures of her in a compromising position with this man?"

I shook my head.

"Then you don't know anything." He pushed the photo back to me, slow and deliberate. "You made a guess, and you guessed wrong."

In the five stages of grief described by Elisabeth Kubler Ross, denial was a natural first step. "I found a pill bottle in your house and—"

He held up his hand, reminding me eerily of the way one of my law professors used to stop students when they were in the middle of a wrong answer, like he didn't have time for listening to foolish mistakes.

"I doubted Darlene once, when we were in high school. I saw her laughing with another guy on the football team and thought it was something more than it was. Instead of asking her, I acted impulsively and in anger. It hurt people." He pushed his glasses up more securely on his face. They looked even smaller next to his meaty fingers. "That's not something I'm willing to do again until I hear it from Darlene or you give me better evidence than a picture of a random man. That means I won't agree to you putting her on the stand and trying to make her look guilty in front of everyone, either."

Our whole defense at this point was built around his illness. Without proof of a motive, I couldn't prove that Clement's medications had been swapped. Without proof they'd been swapped, any competent prosecutor would argue he'd been faking his condition. As soon as that happened, any chance of an acquittal evaporated, and given the violent nature of the crime, Clement would go to prison for the rest of his life.

All to protect a woman who looked like she'd cheated on him and tried to kill him.

My dad liked to say that some clients lost their own cases. I hadn't really understood what he meant until this moment. If Clement wasn't such a large man, I would have been tempted to try to shake some sense into him.

I tucked my hair behind my ears. It was a self-soothing move, and I knew it, but hopefully Clement wouldn't pick up on it. It helped me stay calm.

I had to make sure he understood the potential consequences without putting us even further at odds. He didn't have to keep me as his lawyer. He could fire me.

And for reasons beyond wanting to see justice done, that thought twisted me up inside the same way I felt when I thought I might be audited for my taxes. I didn't want to lose this case. This was my case to prove I could do this job. Losing because my client gave up felt like a bigger failure than losing because the prosecution out-argued me.

"I can't win your case if we can't point to who tried to kill you by switching out your meds," I said softly.

I made sure not to say *if we can't point the finger at Darlene and she's guilty*, even though I wanted to. There was a chance I wouldn't be able to find concrete enough evidence to convince Clement. He'd be more difficult to convince than a jury would. He needed more than reasonable doubt. He needed certainty.

"You can point to that person," Clement said. "You just can't point to Darlene."

In a strange way, his loyalty reminded me of Mark. Even when Mark thought I was interested in someone else and didn't want to be around him, he'd still made sure I was safe because he cared about me.

Clement pushed his glasses down again and rubbed the spot on his nose where they normally sat. "You're not married yet, so maybe you can't understand this, but you have to believe in the person you're spending your life with. You have to see their best qualities when no one else does, and you have to defend them when anyone tries to tear them down."

He was right. I'd seen too many couples who cheated and lied. I'd been lied to myself in the relationship I'd had prior to Mark. Trust was something I was still learning, and loyalty was a quality I wanted people to think of when they thought of me. If Mark were ever accused of something horrible, I hoped I'd stand by him and defend his innocence even if no one else did.

Clement left me with only one choice—I had to prove beyond more than a reasonable doubt that Darlene had motive and had acted on it. Because now, I couldn't stand to accuse her either until I was completely sure.

$\mathcal{I}$ didn't have access to Darlene's medical records and prescription history or the ones belonging to her mystery man, but I might be able to subpoena a list of their prescriptions if I could identify what was in Clement's pill bottle. If either of them had a prescription that matched what Clement was being given, it should be proof enough even for Clement.

I broke the speed limit driving back to Fair Haven. Dr. Horton's Pharmacy closed at 7:00 pm. If I had any hope of getting the records in time for Clement's arraignment, I had to see Saul tonight.

The pharmacy door didn't open when I tugged on it. I checked my watch. Five minutes to 7:00 pm. Saul must have started to close up early, but if he knew I was out here, surely he'd unlock the door and let me in.

I banged my fist against the glass and prayed that Saul was the one in today. It was my first time coming to the pharmacy since the day he was at his brother-in-law's funeral. If Saul wasn't the one in, the other pharmacist might make me come back tomorrow or tell me to hire a lab.

Telling me what pills were in the bottle was outside of their scope of practice, so I was basically asking a favor to figure out what these pills were more quickly than I could get results from a lab. All I needed was enough to get a subpoena before Clement's court date. Then I would get an official lab report and contact an expert who could testify.

It might be enough to have his case dismissed. At the very least, it would ensure I could enter the results of the lab test and subpoena as evidence.

I wrapped my arms around my body for extra warmth. The streets were dark except for the halos around the street lights. I pounded on the door again.

Saul rolled into view on the other side of the door. I waved frantically and pressed my hands together in the universal sign for *please*.

He maneuvered his chair like a car executing a three-point turn. He turned the door lock, and then moved his chair out of the way.

I hurried inside and stomped my feet. There wasn't snow outside yet, but it seemed to warm up my toes as well.

"What's wrong?" Saul pointed toward the door behind me. "Lock up, please, so we don't get any extra guests."

The mental debate in my head went back and forth between checking in on him to see how he was doing after his brother-in-law's death and jumping straight to the point so that I didn't use up any more of his time than was necessary. Sensitivity versus practicality.

My concern for him won out. "I need a favor, but first, how are you doing?"

He waved a hand in the air. "It's a chapter of my life that's finally closed, and I'm glad to have it behind me." He turned his chair around and rolled over to the counter. "Did you have something urgent like antibiotics to pick up? I didn't see anything come in with your name or Russ' name on it. If your doctor wrote out a script instead of faxing it, I can still fill it now."

The speed with which he switched topics made it clear his brother-in-law was a zone where we weren't close enough for him to share. He'd shared what he had about his sister because I'd asked for his advice concerning Russ. That didn't make us close enough for him to want to go into the complex emotions that surely surrounded his brother-in-law's death. Some people wouldn't even want to share that with those they were the closest to.

No problem. I could respect that.

"No script." I pulled Clement's pill bottle out of my purse. "I need to know what the pills are in this bottle."

Saul rolled around the edge of the counter to where the computer sat. "Did the label peel off? I don't even have to look at the pills if that's the case. I can pull up your name in the system. In fact, if you're due for a refill anyway, I'll just fill what you have on file. Or is this for Russ?"

That's right. Because Saul wasn't here when I came in, he didn't realize I was working Clement's case and had his permission to access his records. He'd naturally assume it was some problem with a prescription for me or for Russ.

I'd need to start from the beginning. "I've been retained by

Clement Dodd as his defense counsel—thanks in part to your encouragement to fight for what I want to do."

Buttering up a resource never hurt. I dug around in my purse and pulled out the folded copies of Clement's permissions. I'd almost taken them out, but I'd been so busy that I'd left them there. Thankfully, since I didn't want Saul to feel like I was asking him to do anything unethical.

I handed them over. He glanced at them, but it seemed almost perfunctory.

I set the pill bottle on the counter next to them. "I can't go into detail about the case, but I need to know what the pills in this bottle are." I held up both hands to stop any objections. "I won't ask you to testify or anything like that. All I need is confirmation of my suspicions so that I can secure a subpoena for other information I need."

Saul's chair rolled backward a fraction, almost like his hands tightened on the wheels unintentionally.

"I'll take a look," Saul said.

His voice held a strange note—unnaturally normal like an actor in a low-budget soap opera.

Saul took the pill bottle and held it up slightly. "I'll be right back."

He placed the bottle in his lap and rolled backward around the island counter that sat in the middle of the restricted area. It was where he usually prepared prescriptions. Like the front counter, it was almost too high. The counter rested at mid-chest level.

He uncapped the bottle and poured the contents out into a plastic tray. He held the tray up and moved one of the pills around with a pair of tweezers, turning it upside down.

He placed the tray back down, wheeled back to the computer, and typed something into the keypad.

He shook his head. "I thought so, but I checked the code on the pills to be sure. Those are high cholesterol medication."

I braced a hand against the counter. That couldn't be right. They didn't match Russ' medications, and the labels said they were identical. "Can we compare them physically? From a supply bottle. Just to be certain."

"They are what the label says they are." His smile congealed on his face, like it'd been made in a mold and couldn't quite hold its shape once it came out. "I assure you."

A quiver started in my chest and fluttered down into my stomach. Something was very wrong here. I knew those weren't high cholesterol meds. Maybe Saul was trying to cover it up because he thought he'd somehow made a mistake. A mistake in medications could get a pharmacist fired.

I leaned slightly to the side to get a better look at where Clement's pill bottle and two pills sat. Something deep inside whispered that I shouldn't have handed them over. He might throw them out to cover up a mistake he hadn't actually made.

"I'm not saying you accidentally gave him the wrong medications. I know you had nothing to do with..." My voice caught slightly. "With this."

My throat felt like I was trying to breathe through an opening no larger than a needle. Darlene wasn't the only person who had access to Clement's medications after they were prescribed. Saul could have swapped the medications out more easily than Darlene.

He had access to whatever medication he would have wanted to swap it with, and he worked alone.

Clement's fatal insomnia showed up in late spring. That would have been shortly after Saul returned from his failed surgery. If my suspicion was right, the surgery was the trigger.

No, not the surgery. The fact that it had failed. The fact that the back problems Saul had been fighting for years were never going to be fixed.

All the pieces fell into place and threatened the crush me like a rock slide. The picture in Clement's house showing his high school football team—a team he'd played on with Saul. His story about his jealousy over some other man from the team he'd seen Darlene laughing with. The action he'd taken out of jealousy—multiple futures he'd said. His actions hurt people. Not just hurt his future with Darlene.

It was possible Clement had done something to Saul that caused his back injury, ending his dreams of a football career. Saul was willing to let it go until that same injury finally stole his ability to walk as well.

If I were right, I needed to get those pills back and get out of here.

I edged toward the end of the counter. "I'm sorry I bothered you and kept you late. I'll grab the pills and be out of your way since they're exactly what the bottle says."

Saul wheeled in front of me so quickly he nearly took off my toes. I instinctively jumped back.

"I'll dispose of them for you," he said. "Medication shouldn't be thrown in the garbage or flushed."

My brain scrambled for something reasonable to say that wouldn't make him any more suspicious. "That'd be wasteful. Clement can still take them."

Saul didn't move. "I can't let you take them since they don't belong to you."

It was a lie. We both knew it. They'd been given to me by Clement—in a manner of speaking, anyway—and so I had every right to bring them back to Clement. Saul must be betting that I'd let it go, even if I did suspect something.

Pushing past a man in a wheelchair seemed wrong, but he wasn't leaving me with much choice. I wasn't leaving those pills behind. They were my only evidence, and Clement's future depended on it.

I dodged to the side around Saul's wheelchair and back behind the counter where he'd dumped the pills into the plastic tray. I grabbed for them, but they slipped out of my hand and skittered across the floor.

Crap!

"Don't go after them, Nicole."

Normally I wouldn't have listened. It's not like he could chase me down if I found them and ran. But a note in his voice—half command, half plea—made me stop and look up at him.

Saul had a gun pointed at me.

24

*S*tall him, the voice in my head—the one that sounded suspiciously like my mom and stayed calm even when I wanted to panic—said. *Stall him and call for help.*

But I couldn't call for help. It's not like Saul would let me pull out my phone and dial Chief McTavish any more than he would let me pick up Clement's pills and the bottle and walk out of here.

I might be able to text. I kept my upper arm still and wriggled my phone out of my pocket. My hands shook, making it harder than it should have been.

"Why would you bring a gun to work?" I tried to keep my voice innocent and naïve. I didn't have to fake a wobble. It did that on its own. "I haven't heard of any robberies in Fair Haven lately."

Saul had the gun in his right hand, his elbow resting on the arm of his wheelchair and his left arm supporting the right to keep the gun straight and level at me. The man wasn't taking any chances of missing if he fired.

"I think you're smart enough to figure that out," he said. "It seems like you've figured out other better-kept secrets."

I lowered my gaze just enough to spot Chief McTavish's name in my text contacts list. My shaking fingers missed his name and hit Mandy's instead.

My throat closed. I'd have to spend too much time staring at my phone to back out of my messages to Mandy and select McTavish. Now I had to decide between risking that—and having Saul shoot me because he figured out I was sending a message for help—or risking sending a message to Mandy and having her not realize the urgency of it.

Meanwhile, Saul was staring at me, clearly waiting for my response. "It's hard to think straight when there's a gun pointed at me, but if I had to guess, I'd say it was to shoot someone."

Nice, Nicole. Get sarcastic with the man pointing a gun at you. My chances of getting out of this one alive didn't seem great unless I could get a text sent for help immediately.

Saul gave a slow I'm-disappointed-in-you head shake.

Disappointment wasn't an emotion I'd expected in this situation. The look on his face dug up the evil voice in my head that told me a disappointment was all I'd ever be. It'd picked a fine time to come back to life after I'd worked so hard to stab a stake through its heart and bury it.

I was panicking again and losing my focus. I could feel it. Now wasn't the time to think about the ways I still fell short of the person I wanted to be. I had to do something. Maybe if I reminded him that we'd been—if not quite friends—amiable acquaintances.

"I'm sorry, Saul. That wasn't kind of me, but I thought we liked each other, and now you're going to kill me."

I moved my thumb onto the keypad on my screen and texted *Help pharmacy gun* to Mandy.

At least I hoped that was what I'd sent. I couldn't afford to break eye contact with Saul now. Hopefully it'd make it more difficult for him to pull the trigger and kill me if he had to do it while looking me in the face. If he told me to close my eyes or turn around, he had another thing coming.

I also had to hope that message was enough for Mandy to call 911. I'd have been more confident if the name I'd hit by accident were Mark's, but his, unfortunately for me, had been higher up because he was the person I texted most often. I hadn't gone with him right away because I'd wanted to save time by texting Chief McTavish.

Saul's upper body slumped slightly in his chair. "I'm not sure yet if I'm going to kill you or myself." He moved his left hand off the gun and wiped his forehead. He brought his hand right back into place. "I bought this gun before my surgery. I wanted a quick way out if things went badly, and at the time, I didn't want to take the risk of stealing something from work to use in case I ended up not needing it. But then when they told me I'd never walk again and the pain would continue to get worse for the rest of my life…"

His throat worked, and red crept up into his cheeks.

My phone buzzed softly in my hand. I pretended to drop my gaze to the counter.

Fun? Mandy had texted in reply.

Crap wasn't a strong enough word. My blind texting skills weren't up to par at all.

Saul swallowed hard. "All I could think when they told me was it wasn't fair. Then Clement came in my first day back to drop off his new prescription for the high cholesterol meds. I decided I wasn't going to kill myself. I wasn't the one who deserved to die. I hadn't done anything wrong. There were other people who deserved to be punished for ruining innocent people's lives."

Other people? Plural? The heat in the pharmacy felt like it'd jumped up twenty degrees.

Dear God, it wasn't just Clement. He'd done this to others as well.

Dr. Horton's was the only pharmacy in Fair Haven, and Saul knew enough about medications to tamper with them for anyone he wanted revenge on. Like putting something useless in his diabetic brother-in-law's insulin syringes. Or swapping out Victor Kristoffersen's blood thinners for a blood clotting medication. He could have killed others, too, that I didn't know about.

And no one would have suspected anything because he'd orchestrated all of it to look natural.

"I wish it hadn't been you who figured it out," Saul said.

That made two of us. Or, at least, I wished I'd figured it out sooner, when I was somewhere safe and could have told Chief McTavish about my suspicions and had him follow up.

Saul raised the gun up a few inches, level with my heart. I sucked in a breath and held it. He lowered the muzzle a fraction again.

I had to keep him talking. He didn't want to kill me. I wasn't one of the people who'd wronged him. I'd been kind and friendly. Maybe I could talk him into turning himself in or delay long enough that Mandy would realize something was wrong when I didn't reply to her.

I put my phone back in my pocket and raised my hands slowly to chest height in a gesture halfway between *don't shoot* and *wait*. "I'm only a few months away from getting married. I just became a godmother to a beautiful little boy, and I want to see him grow up. I don't want to die. I haven't done anything to hurt you."

The gun dipped another half inch, but he still didn't lower it completely. He knew what letting me go would mean for him. He'd obviously worked hard to kill in a way that would be hard to prove and even harder to trace. I couldn't expect him to throw the gun aside and give up at my first plea.

I moved around the counter. He followed me with the gun.

I stopped at the edge and lowered my hands to my sides, trying to be as non-threatening as possible. "I know you're probably feeling trapped, but I can help. I can talk to the police and the prosecutor, and we'll make a deal."

"They're not going to offer any kind of deal I'd want to a multiple murderer." Saul's arm stiffened, his finger tight against the trigger. He slapped the arm of his wheelchair with his left hand. "I'm better off dead than in prison in a wheelchair."

His gaze met mine, and I had the feeling that I realized it at the same time he did.

He was going to kill me.

prayed that whatever officer responded to the scene of my murder would recognize me soon enough to call in a different medical examiner. Mark would never know that I hadn't intentionally come here on my own to talk to a murderer. I prayed that his faith would be strong enough to see him through losing another person he loved rather than letting it destroy him.

The desire to close my eyes so that I didn't have to watch Saul as he pulled the trigger was overwhelming. But I wasn't going to go out that way. Without a fight.

One deep breath and I dropped and rolled backward to the counter behind me. My knee smashed into the edge, and pain burned up and down, filling my head with a roaring sound.

I ignored it and scrambled the rest of the way behind the counter, using it as a shield. He couldn't chase me in his wheelchair. If he moved around the counter island to reach me, I might be able to run for it.

I strained to listen for the sound of his wheels moving, but all I could hear was my own ragged breathing, the loudness of my blood pounding in my head. The fire in my leg made it hard to concentrate on anything other than the pain. Could I run even if I got the chance, or had I injured my knee badly enough that it wouldn't carry my weight?

"It's not going to work," Saul's voice came from the same spot where I left him. "I'll just wait for you."

Three loud bangs sounded on the pharmacy's outer door, rattling the glass.

"Police," Quincey Dornbush's voice hollered. "Open the door."

"He has a gun!" I yelled.

"Last chance," Quincey said. "Put the weapon down and open the door."

I crawled around to the edge of the island counter. Saul had twisted in his chair, looking back over his shoulder in the direction of the door. He might be able to see it from where he was. I wasn't sure.

Please, Lord, let this not turn into a shoot-out.

I could hide behind the counter and probably be okay, but Saul might shoot Quincey and whoever else was with him, or they might shoot him. As much as I wasn't about to let Saul kill me to hide what he'd done, I also didn't want to see him die. Death was final. As long as there was life, there was a chance for repentance and redemption.

Besides, if he was dead, there wouldn't be even a chance of getting him to admit to what he'd done—and that could mean Clement went to prison for the rest of his life.

The gun in Saul's hand tilted like he was about to drop it, then his arm lifted, turning the muzzle toward his own temple.

I screamed and launched myself out from behind the counter. At the edge of my mind, I thought I heard glass shattering, but all I could think about was stopping Saul in time.

My knee gave out, and black dots spun like a carnival tilt-a-whirl across my vision. I smashed into Saul.

His chair shot backward, and the gun's muzzle flashed past my face. Then the chair went over.

I tumbled to the side and hit the floor. Where was the gun? Had Saul managed to hold onto it?

Before I could reorient myself enough to look for it, shouting voices surrounded us, and someone's body blocked my view. At first I thought they were shouting at me, but they weren't. The shouting was over by Saul.

The person in front of me knelt down on one knee, and Quincey's face and balding head came into view, leaning over me, a little closer than was comfortable. His forehead was all scrunched up, and he'd lost his hat somewhere.

"Are you alright?" he asked.

I accepted his help to sit up. Except for how fast my heart was beating and the throbbing in my knee, everything else felt fairly normal. "My knee's hurt, but I did that to myself."

Quincey rocked back. "That's a relief. I didn't want to be the one to have to notify Mark if anything happened to you. I'm not sure he'd go along with the whole *don't shoot the messenger* thing." He climbed back to his feet. "Now, as soon as they get Saul secured, I'll go out and get Mandy. She followed us here and was ready to break down the door herself if we didn't."

26

*C*lement shook my hand hard enough that I felt it all the way up into my shoulder. "I didn't tell Darlene what you thought," he whispered as he let my hand go. "We'll keep that between us."

I mouthed the words *thank you*. It turned out I couldn't have been more wrong about Darlene. She hadn't been cheating on Clement. The man she'd been meeting with was the leader of her grieving spouses support group, for people who had or were about to be widowed.

It turned out there was no knitting group. Darlene had been going to the grieving spouses group and hadn't wanted Clement to know because she hadn't wanted to burden him with how much she was struggling with losing him. She'd been attempting to protect him in what small way she could.

He joined Darlene, who was waiting a little further down the courthouse hallway, and they walked out hand in hand.

I'd laid out all the evidence for the judge, including testimony Saul gave about how he'd given Clement extremely powerful stimulants. He'd been right when he said prisons weren't designed for people in a wheelchair. Given how many people he'd killed, he'd spend the rest of his life in prison. I'd convinced him that he'd be better off making a deal in exchange for some small things that would make the rest of his life more bearable.

Along with the case precedent I'd found for murders committed while people were sleep-walking, that convinced the judge to let Clement go. Both the judge and the prosecutor seemed to recognize that putting Clement in front of a jury trial would be a waste of time. To most people, it'd feel like a victim was being put on trial.

Privately, Clement told me he wouldn't have felt that way. He would carry the guilt for Gordon's death for the rest of his life. Even though he hadn't been responsible for his actions when Gordon died, he had hurt Saul back in high school. Saul had been offered football scholarships from multiple schools. He'd lost them when a dirty hit by a jealous Clement during a practice skirmish seriously injured Saul's back and made it impossible for him to ever play again.

Mark and Anderson came up behind me.

Mark slid an arm around my waist and nodded toward Clement and Darlene. "I hope we're like that twenty or thirty years from now."

I hoped so, too. I'd told Mark about Clement's absolute faithfulness to Darlene and his refusal to even consider she might have tried to hurt him. Not only did I want to be that person for Mark, but I wanted to be able to count on him having that level of faith in me.

"I should go," Anderson said. "I have a lot of work to do."

He had the same clipped tone to his voice as I'd expect if I'd bumped into a stranger on the street because I wasn't paying attention.

I glanced up at him. As a lawyer, he was good at hiding things, but I'd been trained by my parents. The muscles in his neck were too tense, and he wasn't making eye contact.

I hadn't thought I'd done that badly, so he shouldn't be embarrassed to have me associated with his practice. "What's wrong?"

He re-buttoned a perfectly fine button on his suit jacket. "You could have simply told me you didn't want to join my firm as a partner instead of going through the charade of pretending you weren't good in the courtroom."

I felt a bit like I'd walked into a glass door that I hadn't realized was there. I had succeeded in making my case and in getting Clement released. I'd even managed to be articulate most of the time, despite being rusty. "That was better than I've ever done before. I don't understand what's changed. If I could do that every time, I'd feel confident in taking on clients and joining you."

Mark's hand tightened on my waist. "It's because he was innocent."

I couldn't keep my mouth from drooping open even though I could hear my mom in my head. *You're not a baby bird waiting to be fed, Nicole. Close your mouth.*

Mark had to be right. When I'd been arguing in the courtroom, I hadn't been thinking about how many people were listening or even how I sounded. All I'd been thinking about was Clement and Darlene and how they deserved to spend their golden years together. I'd been thinking about how it wouldn't be fair for him to spend time in prison when he hadn't wanted to hurt anyone. He'd thought he was protecting his home from a bear.

When I was working for my parents, I hadn't wanted to defend people who were guilty. Even when I'd been trying to practice my public speaking skills in other forums like Toastmasters, it'd been with the end goal of defending people I knew should be in prison for what they'd done. It was like my subconscious rebelled in the only way it could, given how I felt about making my parents proud.

This time, I'd wanted to win.

I leaned into Mark. I probably should have seen it before, but at the same time, it made me feel very loved that he'd seen it.

I'd be able to argue competently in court whenever I was defending a client whose innocence I believed in. Since I'd made it clear to Anderson those were the only types of clients I was willing to defend, my last barrier was gone.

I stuck out my hand toward Anderson. "I think I will accept that offer. You have yourself a new partner."

BONUS RECIPE: MAPLE SYRUP TRUFFLES

INGREDIENTS:

1/4 cup softened butter

1 tablespoon maple syrup

1 1/2 cups powdered sugar

1 teaspoon vanilla extract

1/4 teaspoon maple extract

1 cup semi-sweet chocolate chips

INSTRUCTIONS:

1. Use an electric mixer to beat together butter, maple syrup, and powdered sugar. It will look sandy when you're done.

2. Add in the vanilla extract and the maple extract. Beat again with the mixer until it turns creamy.

3. Refrigerate for 30 minutes. (Be careful not to leave it for too much longer or the mixture turns almost too hard to work with.)

4. After 30 minutes have passed, form tablespoon-sized balls of

dough. Place them on a cookie sheet lined with parchment paper. (Wax paper will work as well.)

5. Refrigerate for at least another 15 minutes.

6. When you're almost ready to bring them out of the refrigerator, melt the chocolate.

7. Remove the balls from the refrigerator, and coat each individually with the chocolate.

8. Allow the chocolate to firm up before serving.

MAKES 15-20 truffles.

EXTRA TIP: You can use any kind of chocolate you like to coat the truffles. If you prefer a less sweet treat, use dark chocolate. If you prefer a milder flavor, use white chocolate. For more tips on how to successfully coat your truffles in chocolate, you can follow this link to see the great suggestions contributed by my newsletter readers: http://preview.mailerlite.com/p9g2u7

LETTER FROM THE AUTHOR

It's hard to believe that we're now eight books into the series. In Book 9 (*End of the Line*), not only is Nicole and Mark's wedding fast approaching, but the mystery of the ongoing corruption in Fair Haven will finally be solved.

I wanted to say thank you to all of you who've followed along on this journey with me. Your support of this series has allowed me to pursue my dream of writing as a full-time career. I couldn't have done this without you!

You can continue on with the Maple Syrup Mysteries in *End of the Line*.

If you liked *Bucket List*, I'd also really appreciate it if you also took a minute to leave a rating. Ratings and reviews help me sell more books (which allows me to keep writing them), and they also help fellow readers know if this is a book they might enjoy.

Love,

Emily

ABOUT THE AUTHOR

Emily James grew up watching TV shows like *Matlock*, *Monk*, and *Murder She Wrote*. (It's pure coincidence that they all begin with an M.) It was no surprise to anyone when she turned into a mystery writer.

Alongside being a writer, she's also a wife, an animal lover, and a new artist. She likes coffee and painting and drinking coffee while painting. She also enjoys cooking. She tries not to do that while painting because, well, you shouldn't eat paint.

Emily and her husband share their home with a blue Great Dane, seven cats (all rescues), and a budgie (who is both the littlest and the loudest).

If you'd like to know as soon as Emily's next mystery releases, please join her newsletter list at www.smarturl.it/emilyjames.

She also loves hearing from readers.

www.authoremilyjames.com
authoremilyjames@gmail.com

CPSIA information can be obtained
at www.ICGtesting.com
Printed in the USA
LVHW051100090619
620628LV00001B/65

9 781988 480176